DEMON DECEPTION

The Resurrection Chronicles

M.J. HAAG

To cheesecake.
To ice cream.
To all the food I'd miss if the stuff I wrote would ever come true.

What wouldn't a mother do to protect her children?

Cassie's world is falling apart. Grieving from the loss of her husband and youngest child, she lives in fear of losing her remaining daughter. She knows she can't protect her alone. There's a solution, as terrifying and as heartbreaking as she finds it, that will ensure she never has to suffer such a devastating loss again. She needs to sleep with one of the dark fey who rose with the hellhounds. More than that, she needs to become his. She has to give him the one thing she isn't sure she can. Her heart.

Cassie must figure out a way to set aside her grief long enough to get the deed done. After all, what wouldn't a mother do to protect her child? Even risk falling in love again.

Weeks ago, earthquakes unleashed hellhounds onto mankind. The bite of a hound changed humans, turning people into flesh-craving infected.

However, the hellhounds weren't the only things to emerge from the earthen caverns. Demon men with grey skin and reptilian eyes had been trapped underground for thousands of years.

They, alone, can kill the hellhounds and bring a stop to the plague. They only ask for one thing in return: a chance to meet women who might be willing to love them as they are.

CHAPTER ONE

"IT'S BEEN FIVE WEEKS, MATT. FIVE. HOW MUCH LONGER DO you think they'll last?"

Matt Davis looked at me with pity, and the need to scream at the leader of our survivor camp warred with my need to cry because I knew what was coming. It was the thing I'd been trying not to think since the day the old commander killed himself.

"Cassie, you need to ask yourself if there's any hope your husband and son are even still alive. We both know what that answer is. I can't risk any of our number on a hopeless mission. I'm sorry."

My temper snapped, and I slapped my hands on his desk.

"Bullshit. You're not sorry. You're afraid. I'm not. I refuse to give up. I will find a way to get to them."

Matt exhaled heavily as I turned and stormed toward another section of the hangar. Tears fell unchecked until I reached the screened area where I'd left my daughter. My hands shook as I wiped the moisture away. How much trauma was a person able to endure before that person snapped? The idea of giving up, like so many others had, scared me. I knew I'd welcome my own end to escape this new hell I called reality, but I couldn't leave my daughter alone. Just like I couldn't give up on finding out what had happened to Lee and my infant son, Caden.

Taking a steadying breath, I quietly stepped around the screen and checked on my daughter. At almost four, Lilly still napped often. Probably more than she should since all of the sleeping meant she would stay up well after a normal bedtime. Yet, staring at her head of dark auburn hair, the same shade as mine, I couldn't bring myself to wake her up.

Nights were scary at the Whiteman base in Missouri, the only safe zone to survive in the weeks after the earthquakes released the hellhounds and started the spread of the infection. The rows and rows of tents for the survivors set up near the back of the base did nothing to help us feel safe. Every howl and groan that echoed through the night kept a sane person awake. Lilly, even as young as she was, didn't sleep heavily anymore. There'd been too many breaches in the fence surrounding the base. Too many attacks where I'd had to pick her up and run for the safety of the metal hangars. No matter how little I let her sleep during the day, she wouldn't give in to sleep until nearly dawn.

I smoothed back Lilly's hair and stared at her sleep-relaxed face. Would she ever know what it was like to live in a house? Would she grow up sleep-deprived and always afraid? Would she ever see her brother or father again?

Tears started to gather anew, and I quickly moved away from her to look at the meager medical supplies still on the shelves.

Being shoved into the role of the camp's only doctor did have its perks. No one had questioned me when Lilly and I had started sleeping in the makeshift medical clinic. She had fewer nightmares with the thin metal walls of the hangar surrounding her. Not that they offered much more protection against what lurked outside the fence day and night.

Footsteps reached my ears, the familiar cadence growing in volume as Matt approached. I quickly moved from where my daughter slept and pretended to count the supplies on the shelves, not that there was much to count. I'd used just about everything we'd had almost a week ago on one of those unnerving creatures that now existed in our world. The dark fey looked more like demons than creatures of magic. Unnatural grey skin and eyes that looked like they belonged to a snake sent a shiver of fear through me every time I saw one of them.

"Mrs. Feld."

I cringed. Matt only called me that when he needed me to be the camp doctor. Otherwise, I was Cassie, another pain-in-his-ass survivor.

I turned slowly and fought not to flinch at the sight of the demon standing next to Matt. As the camp doctor, I usually managed to avoid them, a task that had gotten easier once their leader moved them to a new demon-only safe zone not far from Whiteman.

"Another one of Molev's men was hurt last night. Molev is requesting your assistance at Tolerance."

Although I kept my gaze focused on Matt, I still saw the demon's lizard-like eyes locked on me with an intensity that made my stomach churn. Along with hearing what they were, dark fey imprisoned in the ground thousands of years ago, I also heard they had a thing for human women because they didn't have their own.

"I can't," I said calmly. "It's not safe for Lilly outside the fence. If the patient comes here, I can attempt to treat him."

"I'll keep an eye on Lilly," Matt said, his expression hardening. "The fey need our help, Mrs. Feld, and we will give it. Grab what you need. You leave immediately."

My stomach twisted, and panic burst in my chest.

"You can't do this, Matt. I will not—"

"I'd like to speak to Mrs. Feld alone," he said, looking at the dark fey.

The demon's gaze swept over me before he turned and left. I stayed where I was and tried to control the shaking that wanted to consume me.

Matt crossed the area and lowered his voice.

"We can't say no, Cassie. The fey have given us a lot and asked for very little in return. If we don't make an effort to reciprocate, we run the risk that they'll stop helping altogether. We won't last long without them."

"And how much do you expect me to give?" I said angrily, careful to keep my voice down. "I've helped every time you've asked even though I'm not a doctor or even a registered nurse. I was a fucking student, Matt. I've done more than half the people here have, and now you're sending me out there? Outside the fence where you just told me it was too dangerous to send any of your people? I asked for your help, and you wouldn't give it. Screw you, Matt. I'm not leaving my daughter."

"We need them, Cassie. The food they bring. The protection they provide. They're not asking for a lot. Just your help trying to fix one of them up. You've already done it once. You can do it again."

I thought of the demon I'd stitched up almost a week ago. Attacked by a hellhound, I hadn't thought he would live. The entire time I'd stitched him, my hands had shaken with the knowledge of what I risked. Hellhounds spread the plague. One bite, and a human became a mindless zombie. And, I'd been forced to work on his saliva-coated body.

"Hellhounds are the only things I've seen that hurt them," I said. "I risked my health once. I won't do that again. I'm all Lilly has."

"You don't have a choice. You help them, or I kick you and your daughter out. We all pull our weight here."

Stunned, I stared at him for a moment.

"You wouldn't," I said.

"I would. I'd hate myself for it, but I can't put the needs of one before the needs of every other person within this fence. I'll stay with Lilly until she's up then take her to Bertha. She'll be safe in the kitchen and well-fed until you get back."

Since the moment the first hound howled outside our home, it had been just Lilly and me. The world had gone to shit in hours, and everything had changed. My son, only eight months old, had been with my husband, Lee. I had no idea what happened to them. And now, safely inside Whiteman's fence, the question of their fate was eating me alive. I needed to know. But, I couldn't leave the base on my own. Outside Whiteman's fence, infected roamed, waiting for prey during the day. At night, nothing moved but hellhounds. And only moments ago, Matt had insisted it was too dangerous for a group too. Yet, here he was, forcing me out.

Yep, the world had gone to shit, and the people weren't very far behind. My fingernails dug into the palms of my hands with the anger I felt toward Matt.

I glanced at Lilly while I shook and wondered, again, just how much one person was meant to endure.

"Anything happens to her, and I'll be the only person you'll need to worry about," I said lowly.

Without looking at Matt, I walked toward the opening of the screened area designated as a medical ward. Each step I took from my daughter felt like I was tearing out my own insides.

I rounded the corner and came up short at the sight of the demon standing there. My skin prickled under the scrutiny of his freakish eyes.

For Lilly, I swallowed my fear and forced myself to meet his gaze.

"Can you tell me about the, uh, person who's hurt so I know what supplies I'll need?" I asked.

"Kerr is out gathering what you might need," the demon said. "May I carry you, Mrs. Cassie Feld?"

My heart started to pound, and a shiver raced through me.

"Carry me? Why?"

"Shax can get you to Tolerance faster and safer by carrying you than we can in a truck," Matt said from behind me.

The demon's gaze never left me as he waited for my answer.

"I need just a moment." I turned and fled to the bathroom.

Bracing my hands on the sink, I let my head hang as my stomach pretended I was in a boat on a wind-swept sea. I gulped in air, trying to keep it together.

It wasn't just the eyes freaking me out. Several times, infected had breached the fence, and I'd seen what the demons could do. With barely any effort, they could pull a head clean off a body. The strength in their arms didn't make me feel safe; it made me very aware of my own mortality. I couldn't help but feel that humans had no place in this new world.

A sharp knock startled me from my thoughts.

"Time matters, Mrs. Feld. You don't want to be out past dark."

My knees felt weak with that reminder.

"I understand." I took another deep breath and opened the door.

The creature was right there, watching me again. Heart hammering, I gave the answer Matt expected.

"I'm ready."

I barely withheld my flinch when the demon reached for me. A moment later, I was up in his arms. I tried to tell myself to be grateful that this one at least wore a shirt. When they'd first arrived, they'd only worn pants and their leather calf boots and appeared to be completely unfazed by the cold.

The human survivors at Whiteman were very affected by the weather. The brutal Missouri winter, coupled with failing power and limited portable woodstoves, meant that we survivors kept our outerwear on at all times.

"I will return Mrs. Feld before dark," he said to Matt.

"Keep Lilly safe," I added, hearing the tremble in my voice.

Matt nodded, and the demon took that as a dismissal. As he walked toward the exit, he watched as I struggled with where to put my hands. Finally, I set them on my lap and looked toward the door.

"It's snowing," the demon said. "You need to put your hood up."

Listening to the demon's advice, I pulled up my hood before he held me with one arm as he opened the door. Bothered by the ease with which he bore my weight, I tried to focus on the tiny flakes drifting in the air. It didn't help.

As the creature ran the distance to the main gate, I could feel his gaze still on me, and my already fluttering pulse picked up in speed.

Going outside the fence terrified me. Not only were there things out there that wanted to kill me, but I'd be alone with a demon whose kind only remained on the surface for one reason. Women.

I shuddered harder.

"Are you too cold, Mrs. Cassie Feld?" he asked. "Should I wrap you in a blanket?"

And prevent me from moving? Hell no, I thought to myself.

"I'm fine. Just a little nervous about going outside the fence."

"I will keep you safe. I promise," he said.

The guards at the first set of gates watched our approach.

"Where are you going, Mrs. Feld?" one of the men asked. He had his hand on the firearm strapped to his waist. Not that it would do any good. The grey men moved much too quickly to purposely hit them.

"Tolerance," I answered. "Matt ordered me to help a wounded...person there."

The guard looked at the demon holding me.

"Wouldn't you rather ride in a truck?"

"Matt didn't give me that option," I said, not bothering to keep the bitterness from my tone.

"I will keep Mrs. Cassie Feld safe," the demon said to the guard.

"See that you do."

The grating sound of the gate opening made my stomach churn. As soon as there was enough of a gap, the demon slipped inside the pen. We waited for the first gate to shut and the outer gate to open.

"The wind will take your breath," the demon said. "It is okay to hide your face."

I wasn't sure what he meant until he started running. Wind battered my face and stung my eyes.

Unable to breathe, I turned my head toward his chest. I couldn't bring myself to tuck my face against his shirt, though.

While I was grateful for the coat I wore, I wished I had gloves, too. My fingers began to ache with the chill as the minutes passed, and I curled them into fists and tried to use my sleeves to hide my skin.

My stomach dipped as the creature jumped suddenly, and I looked up just in time to see him slip over a towering wall made of upright vehicles and other debris. The demon landed with a soft thump on the snow-covered grass just inside the barrier.

"Thank you, Shax," a woman said, drawing my attention. "You can put her down now."

He did as she said. Nervously, I glanced over the area. Other demons walked around between houses and along the wall that ran as far as I could see in each direction. I didn't see or hear a single infected, though.

I looked at the woman who'd spoken. Her dark hair was streaked with strands of silver. Unlike so many of us at Whiteman, she didn't have dark circles under her kind, brown eyes.

"You're completely safe here, Mrs. Feld," she said. "The fey built this wall to keep the infected out. It's much sturdier than the fence at Whiteman. Not a single infected has breached it. Not that they've really tried. They know the fey are here, so they tend to stay away." She gave me a friendly smile and motioned for me to follow her.

The fey who'd carried me trailed behind us as we followed a path through the backyard of a nice two-story home.

"We're very grateful you were able to come," she said. "I know it can be a bit terrifying leaving the fence. How is your Lilly?"

The mention of my daughter renewed my anger with Matt and had me glancing at the woman's profile again.

"Do I know you?" I asked.

"Not really. My husband, son, and I lived at Whiteman before Mya and the fey found us. I'm Julie, Mya's mother."

"Ah." I remembered the girl showing up with the horde of demons in tow, introducing a new level of fear to my hell.

"I'm sorry if I sound rude, but can you just show me to the one who is hurt? I want to get back to my daughter as soon as possible."

"Of course."

Julie led me to the nearest house and opened the back door. Warm air enveloped me as I stepped inside.

"You have heat?"

Julie grinned.

"The gas lines still work. The men are fitting all the houses with wood stoves just in case, though. Go ahead; take off a few layers. You won't need them in Tolerance."

I stripped out of my coat and an extra sweater as I looked around. The interior was nothing like the damaged, bloodstained homes on the base. Fresh, neutral tones of paint coated the walls, and tasteful pictures depicting a variety of outdoor scenes hung in various places. It felt surreal to be standing in such a normal looking kitchen.

"Merdon, the fey who's hurt, is back here with Kerr," Julie said, once again leading the way.

I followed her to a bedroom with three fey in it.

The giant standing beside the bed looked up at me, and my feet froze in the doorway while my heart tried to beat its way out of my chest. His eyes and the small scars that crisscrossed his face made him fiercely terrifying. My hands started to shake.

"This is Merdon," Julie said, leaning over the creature on the bed and gently smoothing back his hair. "He was attacked by several hellhounds."

Scratches, gashes, and puncture holes littered the skin of his exposed torso. A few of the wounds oozed, but none of them bled. His chest barely moved with each shallow breath. He didn't look good, just like the one they'd wanted me to patch up the last time. It was a nerve-wracking experience I'd hoped not to repeat, mostly because of the imposing demon who'd stared at me during the whole procedure.

The second, conscious demon in the room moved, calling my attention. I looked up, and my eyes widened as I stared at a creature with a familiar bright red bead decorating the end of his right temple braid. My hands started to shake. Him.

"I found some supplies," he said, picking up a plastic bag from the floor. "You'll have enough this time."

I heard the threat in those words and wanted to cringe.

He'd been there when I'd tried to tell them there was no point in helping the other demon. He obviously still held a grudge.

"Kerr has more supplies in the living room," Julie said, oblivious to the undercurrent as she straightened away from the injured demon. "Suture packages, bandages, alcohol, iodine, and more. Kerr must have been watching you closely when you stitched up Ghua. These men sure pay attention to the details.

"We'll give you some room to work. I'll just be in the kitchen. Shout if you need anything."

She walked out of the room, and the giant trailed behind her.

Left alone with the demon who'd been tormenting my brief dreams for the last week, I couldn't look away from his snake-like gaze. Why him?

He lifted the bag of supplies higher.

"Heal him."

CHAPTER TWO

Do what you need to do to keep Lilly safe, I thought. Just pretend this creature is human. A bossy, asshole-prick like Matt.

I took a slow breath, swallowed hard, and grabbed the bag from him.

"I'll do my best," I said.

Facing the bed, I studied the injured fey. His grey skin seemed a shade darker than the rest of his kind. Normal or a sign of something going wrong? I leaned over the fey and examined the wounds on his chest. Black scabs covered the majority of them, and the skin around a few of them appeared near black.

"I'm not sure how much I can do for him, even with supplies. These injuries look a few days old and well on their way to being healed."

I reached out to check his skin's temperature, but the fey with the bead in his hair caught my wrist, making me jump.

"He was attacked by hellhounds. Use the gloves in the bag."

I nodded quickly, and he released me. My anger and resentment grew by the moment. Fucking Matt. Fucking hellhounds and zombies. Fucking Lee. He should never have taken Caden out that night.

Looking in the bag, I found a box of large, non-latex gloves, sutures, bandages, and a bottle of iodine. I wished for the millionth time that I hadn't gone back to school. The only reason I'd done it was because Lee hadn't been happy with the idea of me being a stay at home mom. He'd wanted to live with a dual income and persuaded me into nursing, because of the pay, only a year and a half after Lilly's birth. Why had I given in?

I pulled on the gloves and carefully began to check the visible wounds on the injured demon's chest. I hadn't minded helping people but never had a calling for it. It had taken a lot of time and studying to learn what I had during school. That meager knowledge had tripled in the last few weeks through some trial and error health practice. Again, not by choice. Thankfully, no one had lost their life yet because of my uneducated care. I hoped the current patient would help me out and live, too, because I didn't doubt that Matt would follow through with his threat to kick me out of Whiteman.

I took another slow, steadying breath to calm the anger over the fact that Matt expected me to do everything he wanted while not even considering my request for help. It wasn't like leaving with a few men would be fruitless to him. Whiteman was in desperate need of medical supplies. I could help scour rural clinics for what was needed while also searching for Lee and my son. All Matt needed to do was ask the demon leader and offer him the right incentive. These creatures didn't need our help. They rarely got injured. Although, when they did, they went all out. But, I'd seen how they behaved around females. They wanted women. All Matt needed to do was—

I froze as I understood what I had to do.

I'd witnessed how the demons stared after the women. How they went out of their way to protect them. Any one of these creatures would do anything for a woman who willingly committed to him. In fact, several women were already in serious relationships with a few of the demons. The women lived with them. Slept with them. And, they got just about anything they wanted. I was standing in the proof of that. A nice, heated house in a safe neighborhood.

If I wanted to find out what happened to Lee and my son, all I needed to do was give myself to a demon. My chest tightened, and I could barely breathe as I imagined having to have sex with one of these monstrous men.

My gaze shifted to the face of my patient. His eyes, now open and glassy, locked with mine. How long had he been holding perfectly still as I examined him? How long had he been watching me?

If just their gazes scared me stiff, how would I ever be able to touch one?

"Close your eyes, Merdon. You're scaring her," the one with the bead in his hair said.

The creature on the bed immediately closed his eyes.

I swallowed hard and mentally shook myself. Too much was riding on my ability to help the dark fey. I couldn't screw this up.

"No. It's all right. Can you tell me how you feel, Merdon?"

"Tired. In pain," he said, not opening his eyes.

"Does any wound hurt more than the others?" I asked.

"The one on my right thigh."

My gaze shifted to the sheet covering him from toe to waist. The unmistakable outline of his penis laying to the left made my eyes pop. The thing under the covers looked like a baby's arm. I desperately wanted to run for the door and forget my dumb idea about getting the demons to help me.

You can do this, Cassie. Think of what's at stake. He's injured and needs help. Don't help him for Matt and the rest of Whiteman. Help him for yourself. For Lilly and Caden. Maybe the more you learn about these creatures, the more comfortable you'll become. Then, you'll be able to do what needs to be done without screaming your head off.

"I can do this," I said under my breath.

Moving toward the end of the bed, I carefully untucked the sheet and eased it back to reveal a massively muscled thigh. All my thoughts and concerns about seeing things I shouldn't fled at the sight of black lines running from the skin exposed at the edge of the sheet to his mid-calf.

I nudged the sheet back further and found the source of his pain. A large gash, still slowly oozing blood, just inside of his right thigh.

"Merdon, I need to clean this wound. It's not healing like

the others." I dug through the bag for what I thought I might need and eased his thigh toward the edge of the bed so I could see better.

I looked up at the other fey.

"This might hurt him. Can you keep him still? I don't want to make the injury worse if he jerks while I'm working."

He looked at the resting fey, who'd opened his eyes again.

"Don't move."

My mouth dropped open a little. Although he'd said the words without any tone, it didn't change his cold manner.

The injured fey nodded.

"I will not move."

I set my gloved fingers on Merdon's leg.

"If it starts hurting too much, let me know."

He closed his eyes again. Leaning forward, I gently probed the skin. Just beneath the surface, I felt a lump.

"I need some water. Or alcohol if you happen to have any," I said without thought. "I need to rinse this."

A bottle of alcohol appeared in my peripheral. I grabbed it and started rinsing, my focus on the object, not so much on the patient. Whatever was under the skin was definitely foreign. I set the bottle aside and prodded the edges of the wound apart.

A spray of black blood shot out, just missing my face and coating the sheet.

"Stop." The commanding voice made me pause.

I glanced at the patient, who was silent and holding perfectly still. Then, at the other fey, who stood beside me, only inches away.

"I can't stop. There's something in there. I can see the edge of it." I leaned forward, ready to try again.

Hands gripped my waist, and I was moved two feet from the bed. With wide eyes, I stared at the fey who'd lifted me like I was a piece of damn paper.

"What is your name?" I asked, trying to sound stern.

"Kerr."

"Kerr, if I don't remove whatever is in that wound, the infection will spread. It might already be too late to save his leg."

Kerr took a clean bandage from the tray near the bed and lifted it to my forehead. He wiped my skin and showed me the dot of blood on the white material.

"He was attacked by hellhounds. Whatever is in that wound could infect you. Tell me what to do."

I nodded, shaken that I hadn't even felt the blood land on me.

"Clean your hands with the alcohol," I said. I would have told him to put on gloves too, but they would have never fit him.

Once his hands were clean, I continued.

"There's a lump just under the skin, here." I took his hand and gently set his fingers on the lump. "If it's a foreign object, which I think it is, it needs to be removed and the wound thoroughly cleaned. See these lines running from the wound? In humans, it means blood poisoning. But, I don't know if it means the same thing for your kind."

"Step back," he said.

I took a step to the side, still in a position to watch but out of the danger zone.

Kerr opened the wound with one hand and dug his fingers inside with the other in a detached manner that made me cringe.

"Be gentle," I said. "The infected tissue can be more sensitive to pain."

He grunted and pulled out a blood-coated tooth. My chest tightened at the sight of the large, jagged spike.

"Is that from a hellhound?"

"Yes." Kerr set the tooth on the bedding, glanced at me as if making sure I wouldn't grab the thing, then started dousing the wound with alcohol.

I moved toward Merdon's head.

"As soon as we're done cleaning that wound, I'll bandage it."

"No. I will bandage it," Kerr said.

"I would stitch it," I said over Kerr, "but with the infection, I think it's safer to leave it open."

"Do what you must," Merdon said without opening his eyes.

While Kerr worked on the infected injury, I looked over the other wounds, gently probing any that had the same dark coloring as the infected one. My focus drifted between healing the fey, which would ensure mine and Lilly's place at Whiteman, and what I would do if I did convince a few of these guys to help me. I wouldn't be able to take Lilly with me to search for Lee and Caden. It wouldn't be safe. And, I wasn't sure I trusted her at Whiteman without me.

When Kerr and I finished with everything on Merdon's front, Merdon rolled over so I could work on his backside. It took a long time to gently probe each puncture hole without a scab or with dark skin surrounding it. Finding no lumps, I started disinfecting and bandaging where needed.

Kerr stayed uncomfortably close, quietly handing me whatever supplies I needed. It took longer than I anticipated to bandage each wound, and my lower back ached from the time spent leaning forward. I only hoped I'd done enough to help.

"That's the last one," I said with a light touch to Merdon's back. "Rest, and make sure you drink plenty of fluids over the next few days."

"Thank you," he said.

When I turned to leave, Kerr blocked me. He reached for my hand, and I automatically pulled back.

"No," he said firmly.

Heart hammering, I held still and let him lift my hand. He carefully peeled off the glove, tossed it into the plastic bag he'd been using to collect the garbage, then reached for the other one. Once he had the gloves, he pointed toward the door.

"The bathroom is the next door. Go wash."

I quickly escaped the bossy fey and closed myself in the bathroom.

With a clinical thoroughness, I scrubbed my hands and my face and hoped it was enough. Drying with a clean towel, I studied the tired circles under my eyes. How long had it been since I'd had a decent night's sleep? More importantly, would I ever have another one again? Probably not. Especially if I moved forward with the crazy plan still floating in my head. Could I really sleep with one of the fey in order to find out what had happened to my son? In that moment, I knew I would. I would do anything if there was even a slim chance he was still alive.

Heartache and anger filled me, yet again, for allowing Lee to take him. Eight months wasn't too young to be away from a mother. But, it was far too young to meet a father's new girlfriend.

I looked down and twisted the rings I still wore on my left hand. I should have taken them off long ago; the moment Lee asked for a divorce. But, some stubborn part of me refused to do so until the divorce papers were signed.

The illusion that there was still something to save had faded long before Caden's birth. The pregnancy had been the only thing that had kept Lee from filing sooner. He hadn't wanted our friends and family to think less of him for abandoning me when "I needed him most." He had never understood that telling me he wanted a divorce and then hanging around just to keep up appearances had hurt me more than simply leaving would have. I'd been on my own long before the earthquakes.

Hanging the towel up, I thought back to the moment I'd handed our son over. I should have lied and said he was sick, too, like Lilly had been. I would never regret anything more in my life. Not even what I was about to do.

Taking a deep breath, I got serious about my plan. How would I choose which fey? Definitely not the scarred, scary one. The injured one was probably more the speed I could handle. But, probably not. The way he'd held so still without a single flinch spoke volumes about his strength. The image of Kerr, the one with the red bead in his hair, filled my mind. The way he watched me...the way his hands had gripped my waist. I shivered and turned away from the mirror.

No matter who I chose, I'd likely need to deal with more than I bargained for. I only planned to sleep with one, so I needed to figure out which of them had the most friends or influence.

I opened the door and jumped in surprise when I found Julie and another woman waiting in the hall. The woman I easily recognized as the companion to the fey who'd been injured almost a week ago.

"Eden was wondering if you could look at Ghua's stitches," Julie said.

"I think they need to come out," Eden said. "It looks like the skin is growing around them."

I glanced at the window and saw we still had a fair amount of daylight. And, by helping another one, I could put off choosing which demon to sleep with a little longer.

"Sure. I'll take a look."

Julie led the way to another bedroom where Ghua lay completely naked, belly down on the bed. I'd seen it all before while putting the stitches in, but the view had been in increments because of the sheets I'd used.

I pivoted quickly to give him privacy as Eden scolded him for not covering up and came face to face with Kerr. He held up a clean pair of gloves.

"Thank you," I said, pretending like my face wasn't flaming as red as my hair.

"He's covered now," Eden said. "Sorry about that."

"It's all right." I turned and looked at the stitches. "These do look like they've been in long enough. It'll sting a little as I pull them out."

I looked at Kerr.

"Did you happen to find any scissors? They would be small and come in a package like the sutures and bandages."

"Yes. I will get them."

"More alcohol, too, please."

He left with Julie, and I faced Eden, subtly looking her over for signs of abuse as she sat on the edge of the bed near Ghua's head. She looked completely healthy, a little underfed like we all were, but happy.

"No, Eden," the fey said. "I want to use your lap as a pillow."

"I'm sure you do, but that's not happening. I don't trust you."

He lifted his head and looked her in the eye.

"I will not lick—"

She slapped her hand over his mouth and looked at me.

"They're worse than kids," she said, laughing nervously.

"Um...okay."

"You'll get what I mean if you're around them long enough."

"You're covering my nose," came Ghua's muffled words.

"Sorry, babe," she said, removing her hand. "If you don't

say another word while we're here, I'll let you use me as a pillow when we get home."

He immediately put his head down without argument.

"Here are the scissors," Kerr said from beside me. I hadn't even heard him walk in.

I took the package and set to work. Removing the stitches wasn't easy. Ghua's skin didn't want to let go on the first try for a few of them. Kerr helped with several. Ghua didn't twitch or say a word. Eden played with his hair the entire time until I reached his neckline.

"There were a few scalp stitches, right?" I said. "Hopefully, the hair they wouldn't let me cut away didn't grow into the wounds."

"They" actually referred to the fey standing elbow to elbow with me.

"They're super weird with their hair," Eden said. "It signifies their rank. The longer the hair, the more important they are."

Ghua and Kerr both grunted at the same time.

"Yeah, yeah. The longer the hair, the longer you've lived, and the stronger you are," Eden said with a wink at me.

I looked at the length of Ghua's hair, then peeked at Kerr. I hadn't paid much attention to their hair before, but I had noticed very few of them had short hair. Kerr's was longer than Ghua's by several inches. This was the information I needed.

"We're almost finished," I said, snipping a stitch and carefully tugging it free. I dabbed the tiny spots with some alcohol-soaked bandages then stepped back.

Ghua immediately got to his feet, bare assed and very turned on. My eyes widened as he picked up Eden. She grinned and called thanks as he strode out the door. She didn't seem the least bit worried about the man holding her. In fact, she seemed excited by the prospect of being hauled off by a naked demon. I shuddered, unable to imagine it.

A light tug at my fingers had me looking at Kerr. His gaze held mine as he pulled the glove from my left hand. It caught on the rings, and he needed to lift my hand to carefully work the glove free.

This was the moment to find out if Kerr was my best bet.

"Does anyone have hair longer than yours?" I asked, only a hint of a quaver in my voice.

He blinked at me, and his slitted pupils narrowed. My pulse picked up speed.

"Yes. Molev and Drav have longer hair."

The thought of going to Molev directly terrified me. And Drav, I knew, had Mya already.

"Anyone else?" I asked.

He stared at me for a moment before answering.

"A few close to the same length. No one else has longer."

It felt like my insides were climbing out through my throat.

"Are you seeing anyone, Kerr?"

"I see you," he said.

"I mean, are you dating anyone?"

He blinked at me again.

"No."

He didn't do or say anything else.

"Okay."

All I needed to do was reach out and touch him. One touch somewhere simple, like an arm. Then, see what happened next.

However, instead of reaching out, I turned to leave, running like a coward.

"Wait."

He caught my right hand, stopping me.

Feeling faint, I faced him.

CHAPTER THREE

"GHUA WAS ATTACKED BY HELLHOUNDS, TOO," KERR SAID AS he carefully tugged the final glove free.

Unlike the last time, he stayed right where he was, standing before me motionless and taking up far too much space. And, the intense, unblinking focus of his gaze began to make me nervous.

I opened my mouth ready to mumble a reason to excuse myself when I identified the moment for what it was. An opportunity. My pulse jumped at the thought of trying to seduce the dark fey right there and then. The thought of kissing him made my mouth dry. I licked my lips and tried to draw courage from some forgotten corner of my soul. However, the action drew the focus of his snake like eyes to my mouth.

"Kerr." I said his name in the hopes it would make him seem more human. It didn't work.

Trying to play it cool, I placed my hand on his chest.

The muscles under his shirt twitched, but his expression remained undecipherable. Did that mean he wasn't interested?

"Where is your husband?" he asked, taking me off guard.

"Lee?" The reminder of what was at stake settled my resolve, and I slowly trailed my trembling fingers down Kerr's chest. He had to be interested. There wasn't any other option for me.

"I don't know," I answered.

He studied me for a moment and lifted his hand. I thought he would touch me, but at the last moment, he stepped back abruptly.

"I will return you to Whiteman."

Shit. Could he tell I was afraid of him? Was that the problem? I couldn't help my fear when he didn't blink. I couldn't tell if he was angry or not.

Desperation motivated me to step closer.

I opened my mouth, ready to be a little more blatant in what I was offering, but Julie interrupted me.

"Are you hungry, Mrs. Feld? I made something if you'd like to eat before heading back."

Embarrassed at being caught, I quickly stepped away from Kerr.

"Yes. Thank you."

As I followed her out the door, I berated myself for so readily walking away from my chance. I should have told her I'd be there in a moment then taken just enough time to stand on my toes and kiss Kerr. He would have understood that.

"How is Merdon?" Julie asked, pulling me from my thoughts.

"One of the wounds had a hellhound tooth in it. I think Merdon has an infection, but I'm not sure. They heal from things we'd never survive. I have no idea if he'll be okay."

He had to be okay. If Matt thought he wasn't, I didn't know what I'd do when he shoved Lilly and me outside the fence.

Julie chose that moment to glance back at me and caught my expression.

"Oh, honey, you've done your best; that's all we can ask."

"You would think so," I said softly.

"What do you mean?"

"Nothing." She gave me a look I'd often given to Lilly when she wasn't listening. And damn if Julie's look didn't make me squirm.

"It's not nothing. I saw you working in there. You did what you could. Do you honestly think these men would think less of you if something ends up happening to Merdon?"

I hadn't even considered the fey's reaction. Would my lack of doctoring skills negatively influence the possibility of one being interested in me? Was that why Kerr stepped away?

"They wouldn't," Julie said.

Her answer didn't reassure me. Kerr obviously wasn't interested in me for some reason. If it wasn't my bedside manner, then what? I needed him to like me. Now. Today. Things outside the fences weren't getting better. They were getting worse. I heard reports from people who went on our infrequent supply run. The infected were getting smarter with their traps. How much more time did my son have? I refused to believe his time had already expired.

Julie studied me for a moment longer.

"The fey's opinion isn't the problem, is it?"

"No."

Between the patience in her gaze and my desperation, the dam holding everything in broke, and I could feel tears starting to well up.

"I asked Matt for help. My husband and son were away the night of the quakes. I need to know what happened to them. My son is only eight months old. He needs me. If we survived, there's still a chance that they survived."

Tears streamed freely down my cheeks. I didn't know how desperately I needed some comfort until Julie reached for me and wrapped me in a hug.

"Oh, honey. I'm so sorry," she said.

"I don't want your sorry. I want help. I can't go out there alone. I need help to go check where Lee said he was going. I want my baby."

"Of course you do. When is Matt sending men out?"

Her hand smoothed over my back in a motherly way, only encouraging me to spill more.

"He isn't. He told me he couldn't risk lives by sending people outside the fence. Then, he told me I needed to come here." That was the part that was killing me the most, and I couldn't help but start crying harder. "Outside the fence. Like I'm not a person like the rest of Whiteman, just a tool.

Because he's worried if he doesn't help the fey, the fey will stop helping us."

A growl rose behind me, but Julie didn't release me so I could see what was going on.

"You hush, Kerr," she said against my head.

Her hand patted my back before she pulled away.

"I understand why Matt might think the fey might stop helping, but it's not true. I doubt anyone could stop them from trying to assist the people at Whiteman. It was very brave of you to come here to care for Merdon, though. Thank you."

I wiped at my tears and gave her a disbelieving look.

"I wasn't given much of a choice. Come help or get kicked out. Everyone at Whiteman needs to pull their weight. I'm desperate, Julie. I can't stop thinking about my son. I can't give up on my baby."

The woman's face turned red, and her eyes started to water, making me tear in response.

"I understand. Kerr, go get Molev."

He stepped around me, starting for the front door. I grabbed Julie's hand and held her gaze.

"I'm willing to hook up with one of them," I said, before I lost my nerve, "if that's what it takes."

Kerr stopped walking and slowly turned to face us.

"What?" Kerr asked.

Julie waved him away.

"Go on, Kerr."

He gave me another long, unblinking stare then left. She

waited until he'd walked out the door to give me a reassuring look.

"There's no hooking up needed," she said. "Come sit down."

She led me to the kitchen and sat me in front of a bowl of steaming mac and cheese.

"Lilly would love this," I said. I picked up the spoon and took a small bite, not really hungry but smart enough not to waste good food.

"Who's watching her?" Julie asked.

"Hopefully, Bertha by now."

"And before that?"

"Matt."

She made an annoyed sound.

"I know that man is doing the best he can, but he's made more than a few decisions that I haven't agreed with. Living here's been nice." She tilted her head, studying me. "There are extra houses, you know."

I couldn't keep the disbelief from my expression.

"You're saying I should live here?"

Julie shrugged.

"I thought you said I didn't need to sleep with any of the fey."

She snorted and patted my hand.

"Don't let them hear you're willing to have sex. They wouldn't leave you alone then. No, I meant you and your family could live in a house here.

"I think once Molev hears that you'd like help looking for your husband and infant son and that Matt turned you down, you'll have the help you need. Besides, Lilly will be more comfortable here, in a real house with real beds and heat, than waiting for you at Whiteman under Matt's care. Don't you agree?"

IN THE FADING DAYLIGHT, I looked at the upstairs bedroom in Julie and Rick's home. A collection of toys took up one corner with a rocking chair, books, and a twin sized bed finishing out the room. Perfect for Lilly.

"Lilly will be safe and as happy as a toddler without her mama can be," Julie said. "I'll do my best to keep her busy so she won't know how much time is passing."

My head was spinning, and I couldn't shake my disbelief that Molev hadn't even hesitated to offer fifty of his men to escort me to Parsons, Kansas, my hometown. Not only did he willingly offer his men but also a truck so I could gather more medical supplies for Whiteman. Not that I gave a rat's ass about Whiteman and what Matt might need. But, Molev cared.

"There are several other children here," Julie continued, "so Lilly will have playmates while you're gone."

Julie placed her hand on my arm, gaining my full attention.

"You're also welcome to stay here until it's time to leave. That way Lilly can get used to all of us before you go."

My gratitude overwhelmed me for a moment. However, I'd teared up spontaneously too many times over the past few hours to allow myself to do so again. It was a struggle, but I managed to swallow down what I felt so I could speak.

"Thank you, Julie. So much."

"It's nothing."

"No. It's everything."

Movement in the hallway drew my attention. Kerr had stayed close since returning with Molev. He hadn't said anything, but if I'd thought he'd watched me intensely before, how he watched me now made my skin prickle.

"We should leave soon," he said. "The sun is setting."

That sent a jolt of fear through me.

"Yes. Sorry." I focused on Julie. "I'll get Lilly ready tonight, and we will see you tomorrow."

"It's been so long since I could do someone's hair in the morning," she said, leading the way down the hall. "I'm looking forward to having Lilly here. I always found taking care of a little girl so rewarding."

"Mya must have been easier," I said with a small chuckle. "Lilly is—"

My humor left me. Before the hellhounds, Lilly had been a completely different kid. A normal kid, truth be told. Sassy. Stubborn. Prone to not listening. Now, she didn't sass. She was quiet and listened immediately. She'd learned her life depended on it. Fear had changed her. Fear had changed us all.

Julie once more seemed to read my train of thoughts.

"It'll take her a while, but she'll remember how to be a child when she feels safe again."

"I'm sure you're right." I wondered, though, if my

daughter would ever have a chance. The world wasn't getting any less dangerous to live in. Hellhounds eating people and spreading the plague. Infected eating people and also spreading the plague. And the dark fey. I still wasn't fully convinced they posed no danger to us.

I glanced back at Kerr, who was following quietly behind me. There were so many of them in Tolerance. When the dark fey had lived at Whiteman, it'd been easier to avoid them and pretend humans were still alone in the world. Here, they were everywhere.

In the living room, I tugged my sweater on then my jacket. It wasn't until I was fully layered that I remembered just how I would need to return to Whiteman.

My gaze flicked to Kerr.

"Are you ready?" he asked.

"Yes."

He stepped closer, and my pulse jumped.

"Keep her safe, Kerr," Julie said from behind him.

"I will, Mom."

It wasn't the first time he or the other fey called Julie that. She didn't seem to mind the title. In fact, she treated them all like they were an extension of her family. I didn't understand how she could be so at ease around them.

Kerr leaned forward, and a second later, I was up in his solid arms. His heat radiated into me as he pressed me to his chest. I wasn't sure, but I thought I caught the hint of a rumble coming from him.

Before I could worry, Julie chuckled and reached around us to open the door.

"You could have let her walk to the wall," she said.

"No."

That was it. Just a one-word refusal. I looked up at his snake-like gaze then back at Julie, who was shaking her head and smiling. She seemed completely comfortable with the fey, no matter what the situation.

"Be careful," she said. "If you let him, Kerr will carry you everywhere."

Kerr stepped out the door and took off running across the snow-covered lawns, robbing me of breath. Like before, I turned my head toward the man carrying me but avoided leaning in.

Once outside, I could see just how much the light had faded and was glad for Kerr's speed. However, the return run seemed to take a little longer. It felt like he was weaving more than running straight. A distant groan in the trees as we neared the base confirmed it.

I shivered hard, and Kerr pulled me closer to his chest.

"You are safe," he said softly. "We are almost to the gate."

Something brushed the top of my head. I frowned and lifted my head. But, Kerr was focused on the lit entrance he approached. The guards stood on their raised platforms and watched us. Seeing them distracted me from whatever Kerr had done.

A mix of relief and anger filled me at seeing Whiteman again. I was back to the place where I had felt the safest. Now, it was a place I no longer trusted.

"I am returning Mrs. Feld," Kerr called when we were almost there.

The gate started rumbling open, and he slipped inside as soon as there was enough room. The guards stared down at us, and I didn't miss the curiosity in their eyes.

"You don't need to carry me anymore," I said as soon as the first gate closed.

"No. I will take you to Matt Davis."

"You all right, Mrs. Feld?" one of the guards asked.

"She is unharmed but cold," Kerr said at the same time I said, "I'm fine."

The guard nodded to me and hit the switch for the inner gate.

"I really can walk," I said.

Kerr's gaze dropped to mine.

"I promised Mom that I would safely return you to Matt. Matt is not here."

His fingers brushed against my thigh a moment before he lifted his gaze and raced through the opening. He crossed the expanse from the fence to the hangar in less than a minute. Not enough time for me to process what I'd felt.

Matt opened the metal door and stepped out the moment we neared. Just the sight of him angered me all over again.

"Kerr," Matt said in greeting. "How is Merdon?"

Matt completely ignored me and said nothing about my daughter. I wanted to deck him.

"We will talk inside," Kerr said. "It is too cold for Mrs. Feld out here."

"Of course." Matt held the door open, and Kerr stepped inside with me.

The pair's disregard of my presence made me want to hit

something. Preferably a nose. Maybe even a set of testicles. I wasn't sure yet.

"Please set me down." This time, Kerr listened, his moves measured as he bent and carefully put me down.

"Was Mrs. Feld able to help?" Matt asked.

"Mrs. Feld is standing right here," I snapped. "You should ask me, the person who treated the patient, if I was able to help."

Matt glanced at Kerr, who remained silent, before looking at me again.

"Well, Mrs. Feld? Were you able to help?"

"I treated Merdon's wounds as you requested. I have no idea if what I did helped or not, though. I think he might have blood poisoning."

"What do you need?" Matt asked.

I fisted my hands.

"My daughter. Where is she?"

"She's on a cot in the medical area. Bertha's with her. I meant, what do you need to treat the blood poisoning?"

"I have no idea. I'm not a doctor, remember?"

Matt's expression hardened.

"Mrs. Feld, do I need to remind you what's at stake?"

"No. You've made that very clear already, which is why Lilly and I will be leaving for Tolerance in the morning."

I enjoyed watching Matt's expression change to shock. Served him right for trying to manipulate me.

I moved to walk away, but Matt caught my arm. A growl rose behind me. Swallowing hard, I looked up at Matt in time to see his angry expression close off. He met my gaze for a moment before he released me and glanced at Kerr. I peeked at Kerr too, expecting him to appear as angry as he'd sounded. Instead, he was as unreadable as ever to me.

"Molev asked me to speak on behalf of all the fey," Kerr said. "Do not threaten to force females from Whiteman. This is your only warning. And, do not touch Mrs. Feld again. That is my only warning."

My stomach gave a nervous twist. I'd been willing to hook up with one of the fey for help. But, now that Molev had given his word that the fey would help me regardless, Kerr's protectiveness worried me.

"It's okay." I wasn't sure if I was saying it to the two men or myself.

Kerr looked at me and indicated with his arm that I should lead the way to the medical area.

I hurried across the cement floor, the sound of my footsteps loud in the otherwise quiet building. When I rounded the screen, I found Bertha sitting beside a sleeping Lilly. The cook was lightly touching my daughter's arm.

"She seems to sleep better when she knows she's not alone," the gruff woman said, standing.

I smoothed back Lilly's hair, and she moved in her sleep.

"Thank you, Bertha."

"You want me to stay a bit longer?" she asked with a glance at Kerr.

It was no secret that Bertha didn't like the fey. Before Molev's group had moved to Tolerance, the fey had almost cleaned out Whiteman's stock of canned meat. That and any form of cheesy noodles. It didn't matter to Bertha that the dark fey had resupplied Whiteman's food pantry and done nothing but protect the survivors from infected and hellhound attacks.

Before I could answer, Matt walked into the area.

"Mrs. Feld, could I speak to you privately for a moment?"

"No," I said at the same time as Kerr.

Kerr crossed his arms and watched Matt closely.

"Whatever you have to say, just say it," I said.

"As the only person qualified to look after the health and wellbeing of the survivors here, you have an obligation to stay. You could be condemning countless people to unnecessary pain, suffering, or even death without your care."

Bertha's horrified gaze swung to me.

"You're leaving? But why? You can't mean to go live with those creatures."

"Bertha, when people start asking why I left, let them know Matt threatened to kick me and Lilly out if I didn't go outside the fence to doctor the fey today. I'm going to Tolerance because I'm no longer sure my daughter and I are safe here."

"It was a mistake, Cassie," Matt said. "I never should have—"

"Save it. I don't care. The next time you're feeling desperate or cornered, what's to stop you from pulling the same thing? That's why I'm leaving. If anyone here needs help, you know where I am. I'm not refusing to treat people. I'm just refusing to live here."

A howl echoed distantly, and Lilly's eyes popped open.

"Mommy?"

"I'm here," I said, squatting beside her.

"Where were you? I woke up and you were gone."

"I was looking after someone who was hurt. And guess what I found while I was gone? A house that's safe. It has a bed just for you and toys."

Instead of lighting up with excitement like she would have done before the hellhounds, her expression turned to fear.

"Toys aren't safe, Mommy. They make too much noise."

"Not these toys. Not in this house. You'll be able to play, and nothing will hear you."

She shook her head just as another howl rang through the air.

"Mrs. Feld, please consider the hardship your departure will create for the people of Whiteman."

"No, Matt," I said, picking up my daughter. "That's something you should have considered when you made me leave this morning." I looked at Bertha. "Thank you for taking care of her. I think we're going to go pack now."

Matt ran a hand through his hair as I walked past him. Kerr immediately moved to follow us. I couldn't say that I minded the escort this time.

"Mommy," Lilly said softly. "I don't want to go to the tent. I want to stay here."

"We'll be safe, Lilly." I stopped walking and turned enough so she could see Kerr. She'd seen the fey before. Seen what they could do. As much as they disturbed me, I hoped that having one with us would help her feel a sense of safety my presence, alone, could no longer provide.

"This fey's name is Kerr. He promised nothing would hurt us."

Kerr moved closer, looking at my daughter.

"No hound or stupid human will hurt you. Ever. I will keep you and your mother safe. I swear it."

CHAPTER FOUR

The way Kerr looked at Lilly, then met my gaze, made me worry about what would happen once she and I were in Tolerance permanently. For Lilly's safety, I knew we needed to leave Whiteman. I didn't trust Matt anymore. However, I was no fool and knew living in Tolerance wouldn't be all rainbows and sunshine. The fey obsessed over women.

I didn't let on to any of what I was feeling, though. Instead, I looked down at my daughter with a smile.

"You see? He won't let anything happen to us."

She stared up at Kerr for several long seconds then nodded. I took that as permission to continue on.

Outside the hangar, the temperature had dropped with the sun. Lilly pressed her body against mine as I walked in the direction of the tents. I could feel a small shiver ripple through her but doubted it had anything to do with the cold. She wore several layers of clothes like I did. No, it was the hounds howling in the distance.

I wanted to reassure her some more but knew better than to say anything. Not out here. Not in the dark. She knew the rules. We all did. Quiet after the sun sets. That rule hadn't changed with the presence of the fey. They kept us safer, but the hounds still wanted a piece of anything that moved or made noise. Especially humans.

Lilly's shaking grew worse the further we progressed from the hangar, and I regretted that she'd woken up. Not that I would have left her in the hangar under Matt's care. I didn't trust that man any further than I could throw him now. No, I just wished she could have slept through the night for a change.

Shifting her weight to relieve the ache in my arms, I nodded to the people we passed. All of them returned the silent greeting, their solemn gazes watching the shadows and the fey walking beside me. I couldn't help but wonder how long it would take them to find out that I meant to leave. Matt's reaction would be mild compared to some of them.

"Let me carry her," Kerr said, making Lilly jump in my arms.

I smoothed my hand over her back.

"Shh," I said softly, more to him than her.

Lilly put her hand over my mouth, and I gave her a squeeze to let her know I understood. One moment, I was hugging my daughter; the next, she and I were in Kerr's arms. The man took off at a run, crossing the distance from the last of the pavement to the field of tents.

Without asking where to go, he wove among the rows of tents until he came to a stop before ours. He put us down before Lilly fully registered what had happened. I'd registered it well enough though.

I quickly pulled back the tent's flap and ducked inside with Lilly still in my arms.

A soft rustle of noise came from the dark. Terror ripped through me a second before light ignited. I blinked at Kerr, who set the oil lantern on top of the small table in the center of the room. How had he gotten around me so quickly? As soon as I had that thought, I wanted to roll my eyes at myself.

"Why is there no stove?" he asked.

Lilly whimpered but kept her head against my shoulder and her arms around my neck.

"Talking after dark scares her," I said softly. "Please stop."

His gaze shifted to Lilly in that creepy, unblinking way.

Trying to ignore him, I placed her on our cot and grabbed one of the several backpacks I'd acquired since living at Whiteman. When we'd started sleeping in the hangar, I'd kept the hot pink one packed with essentials on a supply shelf there. Something to grab in an evacuation, if there was half a second to spare, so Lilly wouldn't be without a dry change of clothes and a picture of her family. What remained in the tent wasn't much. Just more clothes, which were necessary to stay warm through a Missouri winter.

It didn't take me long to pack up the sum of our existence into the bags. When I turned, Kerr was squatted down by Lilly, staring at her. She was staring back just as hard.

As I watched, she reached out and touched the red bead in his hair. He blinked, pulled the bead free, and picked up a piece of her hair. My pulse jumped, but before I could move, he started braiding the strands together. Stunned, I considered the huge creature capable of ripping heads off an infected with little effort. He gently and neatly twisted Lilly's silky tresses, carefully weaving in the bead near the end. When he finished, the braid hung just behind her ear. She touched it and looked up at him. Without a single word, he'd just shown us both something very important. He might be dangerous, but he wasn't as scary as he looked.

However, neither of us had time to deal with that revelation before a scratch sounded on our tent flap. Lilly's eyes filled with renewed fear, and her gaze flew to me. When the sound came again, along with a polite cough, I motioned to her that it was okay.

"It's probably someone who needs my help," I said softly.

I stood to see who, but Kerr beat me to it. He pulled the flap aside, blocking my view but not the swirl of cold air.

"Is Dr. Feld still here?" a man asked. "I need her to look at my foot before she leaves."

"No talking," Kerr said before he stepped aside.

I nodded to the young man in greeting then glanced at Lilly, who was shaking. I'd hoped to avoid Matt by staying in the tent for the night. But, with news of my departure spreading, this man would only be the first of many who sought me.

"I'll be in the hangar in a few minutes. Please wait for me there."

The man nodded and walked away. I scooped Lilly into my arms, hugging her close. Her trembling little body clung to mine. Without a word, I moved toward the tent entrance.

The cold wind hit me in the face, and I cringed. Hopefully, it wouldn't snow again. Not so soon after the last one. As soon as I thought that, I knew it would snow. Missouri weather was fickle like that.

I'd only taken a few steps before Lilly and I were up in Kerr's arms once more. Although I appreciated getting to the hangar faster, I knew I'd need to talk to him about picking me up without permission. Like Julie had warned, I didn't want him thinking he could do it whenever he wanted. Especially not when his fingers liked to move so much while holding me.

As soon as the hangar door closed, Kerr put us down, and I started for the makeshift medical area. My steps echoed in the quiet.

Lilly lifted her head from my shoulder to look at Kerr, who walked beside us.

"You run really fast," she said quietly.

"I do."

She studied him for a moment.

"Do you run faster than the bad dogs?"

"Yes."

She set her head on my shoulder, seemingly satisfied with that answer.

When I rounded the corner, no one was waiting, and I realized Kerr must have passed the man on the way here. I set Lilly on a spare cot.

"Close those eyes. I want you to try to sleep. Okay?"

She nodded. Her gaze briefly shifted to Kerr, who stood by the entrance, before her eyes closed.

It didn't take long for the first person to show up or a line to form shortly after. I managed to quietly treat four patients before noticing Matt speaking to the next person in line. The woman shook her head without looking at him, noticed I was watching them, and quickly came my way as the prior patient left.

The young, blonde woman looked pale and shaky.

"Hi, Mrs. Feld," she said quietly. "My name's Angel Pratt."

"Have a seat, Angel." I gestured to the pair of chairs I had set up next to the cot. "What's troubling you?"

She sat, smoothing her palms over her legs like she was nervous. I took the other chair and waited for her to talk. She glanced at the opening to the ward where a few other people, as well as Matt, waited.

"I'm sorry it's not more private," I said, keeping my voice soft and low. "Usually I don't have this many people coming here at once. News of my leaving must be spreading fast."

"I want to come with you," she said quietly.

"You do? Why?"

She swiped at her legs again.

"I know you're not a doctor. That there's a lot you don't know or are figuring out as you go. And, I'm okay with that. Some knowledge is better than none at all. And, none is what'll be here when you leave, so I'd rather go with you."

I frowned, wondering why she thought she needed me. Had Matt sent her to talk me out of leaving? If so, she wasn't doing a very good job.

"As I told Matt, although I'm leaving Whiteman, I'll still

treat whoever needs me. I just don't want to live here anymore."

"I know. Bertha's telling people."

"Then, I'm not sure I understand. Why would you want to live in Tolerance? There are a lot of dark fey there."

"Living with the fey is better than living without you."

I studied her for a moment. She looked pale, tired, and underfed like everyone else. Beyond that, there was nothing wrong with her that I could tell.

"Why?" I asked.

She swallowed hard.

"I just hit six months, and I'm scared shitless. The idea of giving birth…"

My insides went cold. Pregnant? In this world.

She paled further, and I reached out to give her hand a squeeze. My heart wanted to break for her and for my son. Babies in this world were a terrifying thought. They were so helpless.

"The only experience I have is from my own pregnancies. I'm not sure how much help I'll be, but you're welcome to join me in a few weeks."

"A few weeks? Why not in the morning?"

"I'm leaving in a couple of days to go look for my husband and son. A group of fifty fey will escort me. While I'm out there, I'll be collecting medical supplies for Whiteman, too." I let that news settle in silence for several long moments. We both knew what leaving the protection of the fence could mean for me, even in the presence of so many fey. There would be no point to her moving to Tolerance if I didn't make it back.

"When I return with the medical supplies, if you still want to join me, I'm sure you'll be welcome at Tolerance."

She nodded, and I could feel the tremor run through her hand.

"Is the baby moving every day?"

"Yeah. A lot."

"Do you know how much weight you've gained?"

"I'm losing weight, not gaining."

"Morning sickness?"

"No. Just not enough food."

"We'll need to take care of that first. I'll talk to Bertha about double servings for you."

"No, I don't want to eat someone else's share."

"You won't be. You'll be eating your baby's share. It's a living, breathing person, too, and counts in the ration distribution. Do you understand?"

She gave me a small smile and nodded.

"If you need anything while I'm gone, Julie in Tolerance might be able to help you."

Angel stood.

"Thanks, Mrs. Feld."

"Call me Cassie. I'll see you again in a few weeks, Angel."

She offered me a small smile again and hurried from the area. When I looked at the entrance, Kerr was watching me, blocking the presences of Matt and the rest of the patients. Not far from the screened opening sat a stack of the backpacks from our tent.

I glanced at Lilly, who'd fallen asleep shortly after the second visitor. Her tousle of red hair stood out against the white pillow case. My gaze lingered for a moment while I thought of her brother and wondered how much he'd grown since I'd last seen him. If he'd grown.

Shaking myself from my thoughts, I faced Kerr once more, only to see Matt at his side. He didn't wait for my acknowledgement to invade my domain.

"Mrs. Feld," he said.

"Please tell me you're not going to beg or threaten again. Both are beneath you."

He sighed.

"You're right. I won't do either. However, I will continue to apologize. My behavior was out of line. You were right about my desperation."

I studied him for a moment, trying to gauge his sincerity.

"What were you saying to Miss Pratt before she came in here?"

He looked down at the floor for a moment.

"My desperation is because I pay attention, Cassie. I know each and every person depending on me. I hold myself personally accountable for their wellbeing."

"Why?"

"Because someone has to. Because no one caring means humanity is throwing in the towel."

"And what does this have to do with your conversation with Angel?"

"I knew she was pregnant and suggested she leave with you." He held up his hand as if he thought I would interrupt him. "I made it very clear that I wasn't kicking her out. That she had a choice. But that I thought she and her unborn child would be safer with you and the fey in Tolerance. She said she's not afraid of the fey or leaving Whiteman."

My view of Matt shifted in that moment. He was still an ass and probably always would be. But out of necessity. He really did care.

"I told her that I would be leaving with the fey to look for my son in a few days. We both know the risk involved with that, and I suggested she not join me until I return. Can you talk to Bertha about giving Angel double portions? The average pregnant woman should gain about twenty pounds. Angel's lost weight."

"I'll talk to Bertha. Is there anything you need to help mitigate the risk when you leave?"

"I don't think so. Molev is sending out fifty fey and a truck. We're going to be collecting medical supplies as we go. He knows we're out of everything."

"Molev is a good man. Will Drav and Mya be looking after Lilly?"

"No. Julie and Rick, Mya's parents."

I waited for him to say more. To try to talk me into staying even though he said he wouldn't. Instead, he held out his hand.

"Be careful out there, Mrs. Feld."

I wrapped my hand in his, willing to be cordial.

"I'll do my best."

He left the area under Kerr's watchful gaze.

The next several hours passed with a steady string of patients. Finally, I looked up and found only Kerr waiting.

"I need sleep," I said, moving closer to Lilly's cot. "If you'd like to sleep on the other cot, you're welcome to it."

I eased myself down beside Lilly's limp form, not waiting for his answer. A jaw-cracking yawn took over as I closed my eyes and wrapped an arm around her. It didn't matter that I had no blankets or that I still wore my shoes. That was my reality now. Ready to move at a moment's notice and always in need of more sleep.

My mind drifted over the day's events in awe. Every day since the quakes seemed like the longest day in my life; yet, today stood out among the rest. Everything would change come morning light, and only time would tell if it was a positive change or not.

"MOMMY, I HAVE TO GO POTTY." Lilly's tiny fingers touched my face, a mix of prod and caress.

"Okay. I'm up." As I rose, I got tangled up in the blanket covering me. I never used a blanket for this very reason.

Frowning, I looked around the room. The overhead light was off and the screens moved so the area was totally closed off from the rest of the hangar.

"I gotta go." Lilly prodded me again.

I kicked off the blanket and stood so she could climb out of bed, too. She scampered toward the screen and stopped short at the last second when she finally caught on that there was no opening.

"Hold on, Lil. I just need to move it."

Before I finished speaking, one of the panels slid back.

Kerr looked in at Lilly then waved her forward. She looked back at me.

"It's okay," I said. "I'm right behind you."

She raced through the opening, veering in the direction of the bathroom. As soon as the door closed, I looked at Kerr.

"Did you do this? Move the screens?"

"Yes."

"Why?"

"Because you needed sleep."

I would have slept the same without the screens enclosing the area but didn't say so. Maybe he thought I'd feel safer with them in place. Shrugging it off, I went back to the screened area for our pink bugout bag and waited in the hall for Lilly to knock on the door to indicate she was done.

When she did, I went inside and handed over her toothbrush and some paste. While I used the toilet, she brushed. My view on privacy had drastically changed when faced with zombies, hellhounds, and fey. It was easier to keep an eye on Lilly when she was within my line of sight.

She waited beside the door for me to finish brushing. Even here in the hangar, she knew not to open it and go out first. In this world, I feared what might lay on the other side of a door just as much as I valued the protection it provided when closed.

I dried my hands and pressed my ear to the steel panel. Everything was quiet. A good sign or a bad one?

Taking a slow breath, I gripped the knob and motioned Lilly back.

I hated doors.

CHAPTER FIVE

THE DOOR OPENED WITHOUT A SOUND. THROUGH THE INCH-wide gap, I peered into the hall. Nothing waited. Exhaling with relief, I eased the door further open and saw Kerr still standing near the screens. I motioned for Lilly.

"Ready for our adventure?" I asked, holding my hand out to her.

"No. I want to stay here."

"I know you do. But I want us to live in the safest place possible. And I think the house I found is even safer than here."

After wrapping her hand in mine, I started toward Kerr. Two other fey stepped into view as we approached. The hulking, muscled trio watched me with an intensity that slowed my steps. Why were there three now? Had they heard I was moving to their town and wanted to get a look at the fresh meat?

Lilly's fingers twitched, and I gave her hand a reassuring

squeeze. If we were going to live with the fey, for Lilly's sake, I needed to get over my caution around them. Easier said than done when I found their size and strength alone intimidating. Never mind their oversized man parts or their keen interest in women.

The men watched our approach in silence. I studied them in return, noticing the differences in the three. Kerr had the longest hair. But not by much.

The bags I'd packed the evening before hung from the two newcomers' shoulders.

"Mrs. Cassie Feld," Kerr said, "this is Shax and Byllo."

"Hello."

The darker-skinned fey squatted down to Lilly's level and held out both fists, palms down.

"My name is Byllo," he said. "Pick right or left."

Lilly reached out and tapped his right hand. He turned it over and opened his fist to show a chocolate pudding cup. Lilly's eyes lit up, and she looked up at me.

"Mommy, can I have it?"

"Yes."

The man opened it for her and did a cool fold and twist with the lid to fashion a makeshift spoon. Lilly dug in.

"I care for Timmy," Byllo said. "He is close to Lilly's age. Julie says that playdates are good for children. Timmy and Lilly should have one."

"Oh. I didn't realize the fey had children."

"We do not. Timmy is human. He was alone, and I saved him."

"Alone?"

Hope burst in my chest. If a toddler could survive even a day alone, that meant my son might still be alive.

"Not alone," Kerr said. "The stupid ones were using him as bait."

Lilly stopped eating and stared up at Kerr with wide eyes.

Byllo stood and glowered at Kerr.

"Do not talk about the S.O. in front of children. It is not appropriate for them to hear. Like the P word."

My mind felt too numb to register half of what Byllo was saying. It was still stuck on the word bait. I knew the infected were getting smarter with traps, but using children? The small bubble of hope withered inside of me. The idea that it might really just be Lilly and me now pierced me deeply. Devastated, I squatted down by Lilly and wrapped her in a hug.

"It's okay. You're safe," I said against her hair. "And I mean to keep you that way. That's why we're moving to Tolerance. I love you, Lilly-bean. More than you will ever know."

"I love you too, Mommy." Her half-eaten pudding cup fell to the floor as her little arms wrapped around my neck and squeezed me tightly.

I picked her up and looked at Kerr.

"We're ready."

His gaze shifted from me to the back of Lilly's head.

"How fast should I run today?" he asked.

"As fast as you can," she said immediately.

He grunted and started toward me. I looked away,

uncomfortable with what I knew was about to happen. His arms slid around me and hefted us up against his chest.

"Tuck your hands against your mother," Kerr said even as his fingers moved minutely on my leg. "Running fast will be cold."

Lilly curled into my warmth. I pulled up our hoods, held tight, and closed my eyes. The temperature drop let me know the moment Kerr stepped outside as did the icy wind. After we cleared the gate, I turned my face against Kerr and waited for the dipping sensation in my stomach to signal the moment we crossed into Tolerance.

Lilly shook the entire time, and Kerr didn't stop until we were at Julie's back door. He set me down and knocked.

Julie answered a moment later.

"It's good to see you again," she said. Her gaze shifted to Lilly, who'd turned in my arms to look at her. "You're just in time for some cocoa, Lilly. Would you like some?"

Lilly nodded, and I stepped inside.

"Lilly, this is Julie. She offered to let us stay with her for a while."

Julie smiled at Lilly.

"You won't need your shoes or all those layers of clothing in here, Lilly. Go ahead and take them off and then you can have that cup of cocoa right there on the table."

She pointed to an actual mug of cocoa that waited with marshmallows floating on top. Lilly's eyes rounded, and she hurried to pull off her shoes. Seconds later, she was perched on the chair and sipping the first cocoa she'd had in ages.

"How was it last night?" Julie asked softly. "I imagine the

reactions were varied when you let people know you were leaving."

"It was pretty quiet once everyone got over their initial panic that I wouldn't be available."

"And Matt?"

"Reasonable and apologetic. He said he regretted how he handled the situation."

"Do you believe him?"

"I do."

"I'm surprised you didn't stay."

"Regret doesn't change what happened. And, I now know what could happen if he's feeling desperate again."

She made a non-committal sound and watched Lilly for a moment. When I moved to take off my shoes, she stopped me with a wink.

"If you'd like to check on your patient," she said, "I'd be happy to entertain Lilly for you."

Lilly didn't even blink at having a stranger watch her. It wasn't the first time I left her with someone because of my doctor role.

"After she's done with her cocoa, I can show her the room she can use and all the toys we have for her."

At that comment, Lilly looked at me, her eyes wide. I nodded and gave her an encouraging smile. She shook her head and slid from the chair. Julie glanced at me in question as Lilly attached herself quite firmly to my leg.

I smoothed my hand over Lilly's hair while giving the older woman an apologetic smile.

"I don't want to be bait." Lilly's words were muffled against my leg but still understandable.

Julie frowned and bent down to Lilly's level.

"Bait? Goodness, no. I promise the infected can't hear the toys in here." Julie's gaze shifted to me. "Where did she get such an idea?"

"Kerr, when Byllo mentioned the boy he cares for."

"Ah," Julie said, her concern fading. "The fey are learning. Every day. Every hour. Bit by bit. Can you imagine coming here and not even knowing a word of our language or understanding our culture? They make mistakes constantly. Things we think are common sense. Like what's appropriate to say in front of others. Unfortunately, even honest mistakes have consequences."

She studied Lilly for a moment.

"I have an idea. What if Lilly and I quietly bake some cookies while you go check on your patient?"

Lilly turned her head up to me.

"We can't make cookies. Bertha said so."

"Bertha probably said that because she didn't have eggs," Julie said. "But the fey are really, really good at getting to the things we can't, and they found some eggs that are still good. And some milk to go with them."

"You found milk?" I asked in disbelief.

"Powdered, canned, and some in single serving vacuum packages. It's amazing what they bring back when they go out." She smiled at both of us. "What do you say? Should we give Mommy some time to check her patient and surprise her with some real cookies and milk when she gets back?"

Her invitation had nothing to do with pushing me to fulfill some obligation to care for Merdon. In two days' time, the hunting party would return, and I would leave. Lilly needed to be ready for that. To be left behind. And she needed to be able to trust someone here to keep her safe when I didn't return that first night.

Julie held out her hand to Lilly. My daughter didn't turn to look at Julie but kept her gaze focused on me instead. She was smart and knew something was up. Or, like so many others, she just didn't trust change to be a good thing anymore.

"I would love to taste a cookie when I'm done. I'm not sure I even remember what they taste like. Go on. Help Julie."

Lilly exhaled heavily, like she would have done in our old life if I'd told her to clean her room, and reluctantly detached herself from my leg. It took everything I had to turn around and leave the house.

On the back porch, I stopped and looked up. Clouds drifted low in the sky, a sign of more snow on the way. My eyes watered in the sudden chill, and I blinked back my urge to cry, which had nothing to do with the weather.

I didn't know what to do. What decisions were the right ones? I feared my drive to find my son would orphan my daughter. Yet, I couldn't just hide where it was safe for both of us and let the guilt and the burning need to know if he was still alive eat me from the inside. I'd go crazy. Not trying would kill me just as surely as an infected.

Taking a deep breath, I started out toward the house I

remembered from the day before. Footprints tracked the freshly fallen snow between houses, through yards, up and down streets. There wasn't a pristine patch left anywhere, and the reasons why stood in the early morning shadows, watching my progress. So many fey.

One of them came jogging my way, his large frame and serious expression intimidating me.

"Drav, get back here!" someone called distantly.

The man's gaze shifted to the side for a moment as he came to a stop in front of me.

"Drav, I presume?" I said.

"Yes. You are Mrs. Feld, the doctor. Will you look at my Mya?"

"I'm not an actual doctor, but I can try to help you. Tell me what's happening. What's concerning her?"

"She says she is fine. But her head hurts, and she won't show me her spots."

I paused for a moment, wondering if I was understanding the situation correctly. He wanted to see her parts, and she was telling him she had a headache? How exactly did that call for a doctor visit?

"I'm on my way to check on Merdon. But, I'd be happy to stop by afterward."

"I will go with you."

I nodded, figuring Mya would probably appreciate the alone time.

Ignoring my new friend, I let myself into the back door of the house Merdon was using. The scarred giant from the day before sat in the living room, watching TV. When he heard me enter, he stood and muted the movie. I couldn't get over how easily they lived in their human surroundings.

"Hello, Mrs. Feld," he said deeply. "Thank you for fixing Merdon."

"He's doing better, then?"

"Much." He glanced at Drav. "We will be leaving today."

"Good. I will tell Molev after Mrs. Feld looks at Mya."

"What is wrong with Mya?"

"Her head hurts again."

While they spoke, I went down the hall to Merdon's room. I found him sitting up in bed, looking at a children's picture book of fables.

"Is this a history book?" he asked.

"No. It's a children's book. It has tales with lessons to help them understand right and wrong. Good decisions and bad decisions."

He grunted and continued to look at the picture of a wolf that showed a funny image of a child in its belly.

"How are you feeling today?" I asked.

"Tired. My leg itches."

"Do you mind if I look at your injuries again?"

He nodded, so I started with his leg. Someone had already changed the dressing. The wound underneath oozed a pinkish clear liquid, which I figured was a positive sign.

"Everything looks good. Don't scratch any of the wounds when they itch. Keep the open ones dry and clean. It would be better if you stayed in bed for another day or two, if possible."

"I will tell Molev," Drav said from the doorway behind us. "Will you look at Mya now?"

"Sure. Let me just wash my hands."

I found Drav waiting by the back door after I finished washing up. He led the way outside and set a brisk pace back in the direction we'd come.

Drav went around the side of a house and let himself in through the back door.

"I brought Mrs. Feld," he called.

"Seriously, Drav. You're ridiculous."

Mya rounded the corner and gave Drav a narrowed eye stare before she shifted her hard gaze to me then crossed her arms. I recognized her immediately.

"Mom thinks you're a decent person, but she wasn't there when you tried to refuse treating Ghua."

I studied the girl for a moment. She wasn't much younger than me. Maybe four years. Yet, I felt so much older.

"Have you always been so narrow-minded?" I asked.

Her brows shot up, and she pointedly glanced at Drav.

"I think I'm the furthest thing from being narrow-minded," she said.

"Then stop looking down your nose at me and try to see things from my point of view."

"Like what?"

"My four-year-old daughter has no one but me. I'm a human mother who can become infected by working on a hellhound victim. If I were an actual doctor who took an oath, I could see where you'd expect me to jump in. But, I'm not. I'm a nursing student. As in, I didn't even finish school. I have no real idea what I'm doing half the time, but even with my limited knowledge, seeing the shape the patient was in, he should have been dead. I was being asked to risk myself, the only barrier of safety my daughter has, for what I considered a lost cause. When you have a child depending on you, you might find yourself being less brash, too."

"So it had nothing to do with him being fey?" she asked.

I glanced at Drav, who was silently taking in our conversation, and hoped he wouldn't be offended by what I had to say next.

"The fey intimidate the hell out of me," I said. "But that fear had nothing to do with my reluctance to treat Ghua. By human standards and with the supplies we had, I was being asked to risk myself for a lost cause."

She sighed and uncrossed her arms.

"Fair enough."

"Will you let Mrs. Cassie Feld look at you now, Mya?" Drav asked.

"She just admitted she doesn't know much," Mya said. "I really doubt there's anything she can do."

"You might be right," I said when Drav opened his mouth to say more. "But why don't we start with you telling me what's troubling you."

"Her headaches are back," Drav said.

Mya rolled her eyes and walked further into the kitchen. While she spoke, she grabbed two mugs out of the cupboard and started making cocoa.

"Drav comes from a world under the surface. It's beautiful and dangerous on so many levels. One level is the crystals they have there. They don't just give light. They're a source of power. Magic, if you're able to suspend your disbelief that far.

"While I was down there, I got sick because of the crystals. It started with headaches, and after a few days, it almost killed me. I think it was some kind of magical poisoning or something. Now, anytime my head hurts, Drav thinks I'm dying. I tried to explain about migraines, but he thinks it's not that."

"Why do you think it's not a migraine?" I asked him.

"Her marks are getting bigger," he said.

"Marks?"

Mya pulled the neckline of her shirt aside to show me a grey patch of skin on her shoulder.

"Part of the sickness," she said.

The grey patch of skin freaked me out but not as much as the lighter crescent shape in the middle of the patch.

"Is that a bite scar?" I asked. "From an infected? How are you still alive? Are you becoming a fey?"

"It is a bite. As for the fey part?" She shrugged.

Thoughts collided in my head. She was immune. Did that mean there might be a vaccine? A way to stop the spread?

"I wish I was a doctor," I said. "Or someone who knew even a smidge about blood and immunizations."

"I'm glad you aren't. I don't want to be turned into a lab experiment."

"You might change your mind the first time you see an infected child. It isn't pretty."

Mya paused what she was doing and looked up at me.

"Your fears made you hesitate. Mine do, too. We're human."

She went back to stirring the cocoa and handed me a mug.

"The chocolate helps with the headaches," she said. "Every time the fey go out for supplies, they look for more chocolate for me. That's why I think these are just headaches. In the caves, nothing really helped."

"And the marks? Are they getting bigger?" I sipped the cocoa and wanted to groan. It'd been so long since I had anything sweet and chocolatey.

"I don't think so," she said at the same time Drav said, "They are."

"Okay," I said, trying for diplomacy. "Let's mark them. Then, in a few days, you'll have a definitive answer on whether or not they're changing. How many do you have?"

"Just two. One on my shoulder and one on my foot."

I kept my expression carefully blank as I looked at Drav.

"Would you mind leaving the house for a bit? It's normal for a doctor to speak with the patient alone for at least a portion of the visit."

He grunted, gave Mya a kiss on the temple, then left.

"What do you want to mark them with?" she asked. "I have pens and permanent markers."

I set my cup aside and met her gaze.

"First, let's find out how many marks you really have."

She paused her search to look at me.

"What do you mean?"

"When you reached into the cupboard, your shirt lifted a little. You have a very small grey mark near your hip, too."

Mya slammed her cup on the counter and yanked up her top to look. The mark was there. Smaller than my pinky nail and easily mistaken for a birthmark if not for the grey tone.

"Shit," she breathed.

She turned around and threw up in the sink.

CHAPTER SIX

Mya and I sat in the living room. I waited patiently, wanting to get back to my daughter but worried about leaving Mya. Shock still painted her features.

"Feeling better?" I asked.

Her unfocused gaze shifted from the big picture window to me.

"I thought it was just headaches," she said.

The three new marks on her body argued otherwise.

"Drav's going to flip out. He already doesn't let me out of his sight for long." She sighed and rubbed her head.

"I'm sorry. I wish I had something to offer. Some nugget of wisdom. But, this is so far out of the scope of things I understand."

Who knew what kinds of lasting effects being exposed to Drav's world would have on her? The marks were an obvious sign that she was still changing. But into what? One of them?

What would that mean exactly? I wished I had the answers to reassure her. I gave her what I could.

"Other than the headaches, you appear to be in good health," I said, trying to keep things positive. "The fever you told me about hasn't returned. Those are both good signs."

"You're right." She took a deep breath and straightened her shoulders. "There's no reason to worry Drav unless the fever returns or I lose my appetite again. Puking in the sink notwithstanding."

"You were understandably upset," I agreed, standing as she did.

"I could use some fresh air. Let me walk you back to my mom's."

"Are you sure you're up for it?"

"Yeah. Whatever these headaches are, I'm not going to let them stop me from living the life I have, for however long I have it."

"Given the world we live in now, that's all any of us can do."

Neither of us said more as we bundled and went outside. The overcast sky and the brisk wind felt oddly welcoming.

A shadow detached itself from a nearby pine and jogged our way.

"She is sick, Mrs. Cassie Feld?" Drav asked as he reached us.

"Yeah, sick of your babying. Cut it out."

Drav ignored her protest and continued to look at me for confirmation.

"Please, just call me Cassie. And I don't know why Mya is

getting headaches. I'm sorry. I wish I did. But if chocolate is helping them, keeping her stocked up is probably the best way you can help her feel better. When I go out in a few days, I'll be sure to grab anything I see that I think might be helpful."

"Thank you, Cassie."

With the amount of relief in those three words, he sounded like I'd just told him she'd live. I looked away, guilt eating at me. It was plain to see that Drav cared for Mya very much. I wondered if Lee had ever felt that depth of affection for me. Given the way he'd quickly moved on, I doubted it.

When we reached Julie's house, Mya let herself in after a brief knock. The aroma of freshly baked cookies made my stomach growl, a reminder that I hadn't eaten anything yet, and it was almost midday.

"You're timing is perfect. Lilly and I just pulled the last batch from the oven," Julie said.

Lilly smiled at me from her spot at the table. A plate mounded with cookies waited in front of her. My mouth watered as she lifted one up to me.

"Want one, Mommy? They taste good." She took a large bite as if to prove her words.

"I would love one," I said. I kicked off my shoes and walked further into the room.

It wasn't until I was at the table that I noticed Kerr standing in the opening between the living room and the kitchen. He held a cookie in one hand and took a bite while watching me.

"Here, Mommy." Lilly shoved a cookie my way. "Julie made milk, too. It's so yummy."

I smiled at Lilly's enthusiasm and took a bite of my cookie. The cocoa at Mya's house had been amazing. However, the warm sugary confection caressing my tongue was absolute bliss. I closed my eyes and chewed slowly. Never. That's when I thought I would taste a cookie or anything else sweet and useless again.

Julie chuckled and pressed a cold glass of milk into my hand.

"Sit down. Enjoy yourself."

Mya and Drav joined us at the table. Mya reached for a cookie of her own.

"If you find chocolate chips when you're out there, please, please bring them back. Oh, the things Mom will bake." She groaned then bit into her cookie.

"I swear that I'll bring back anything chocolatey," I said as I continued eating.

"Out where?" Lilly asked.

I swallowed hard and set my cookie aside. There was no use putting off telling her the truth.

"I'm going to go back to our old house and look for Caden and Daddy. You get to stay with Julie while I'm gone."

Lilly's gaze flicked to Julie before pinning me.

"I don't want you to go."

"I know, honey." I slid from my chair and picked her up to hug her close. "This is like all those times I had to leave to take care of someone. Julie will be here to watch you until I get back. You know what we should do? We should make a list of all the things you'd like me to find for you. Mya already said anything chocolate. What about you? What do you want me to bring back for you?"

She shook her head and lay it against my shoulder.

"A list sounds like a good idea," Julie said while placing a pencil and a piece of paper on the table.

Mya picked up the pencil and wrote chocolate at the top.

"Any nonperishable food items are always good. If you find eggs and butter, bring them back for us to test. Sometimes they're good. Sometimes they aren't," Julie said. She picked up Lilly's jacket.

"Come on, Lilly. We promised to share the cookies once they were done. Let's go for a walk while your mom and Mya make their list. When we get back, we can make lunch."

Lilly rubbed her face against me then wiggled to get down. I watched her get ready then leave with Julie.

"She'll be fine," Mya said. "Mom will keep her busy. And there are other kids here that she'll get to play with. What else needs to go on the list?"

"Baby items," I said, thinking of my son and Angel, the expectant mother. "Diapers, wipes, formula, bottles...all of it. And any kind of medical supplies."

"That's a lot for one set of eyes to look for," Mya said. She looked at Drav. "I should go with."

"No."

"I can't get infected. You're just being stubborn now."

"Not every person is infected," he said. "Some are just eaten."

The cookie settled like lead in my stomach. It'd been

weeks since I'd arrived at Whiteman. I knew the stories and heard reports from those who went on supply runs. I also knew what it had been like in those first twenty-four hours after the hellhounds emerged. Chaos. Death and the spread of the infection everywhere. And I was going back into it. I shivered.

A hand wrapped around my arm, and I was guided toward the chair I'd vacated.

"Sorry," Mya said as Kerr moved away from me. "With all these guys watching out for you, you'll be fine."

I managed a weak smile and a nod.

"I still think someone should go with you," Mya said. "If not me, what about one of the other girls?"

"No. We will not risk any females," Drav said.

Seriously? What was it with men discounting me as someone important? Was I really so expendable?

Mya's gaze met mine, and she winced before shaking her head at Drav.

"Do you know how that just sounded to Cassie? She's female, and she's going."

Drav grunted.

"She is taken."

"You mean because she's married, you're not putting her under house arrest? That's crap."

Mya scowled at Drav and crossed her arms. He sighed and looked at Kerr. I glanced at Kerr, too. He hadn't moved far after guiding me to my chair. His close scrutiny made my stomach go hot and cold.

"So because I'm married, the fey don't care what happens to me?" I asked.

Something flashed in Kerr's expression.

"We care," he said.

"Drav didn't mean it the way it sounded," Mya assured me. "The fey just know that the rules are different with married women."

"They are off limits," Drav said.

I snorted. "It'd be nice if all humans understood the concept of fidelity."

Drav frowned. "What human does not understand this? I will speak with him. Married women are off limits." He looked at Mya when he said that last bit, and she nodded.

I smiled slightly, understanding what he meant.

"There's no guy hitting on me. I'm just being bitter because my husband was in the process of moving on when everything happened. That's why he and my son weren't with us." I looked down at the table. "Lee wanted his new girlfriend to meet the kids. Lilly wasn't feeling well, so I kept her home. I wish I would have put my foot down and kept Caden home as well."

"Men can be such dicks," she said.

"Human males become a penis? How?" Drav asked.

I blinked at his insensitive mockery of the situation.

"No. Not literally," Mya said. "Calling someone a dick can also mean that they're being mean and unreasonable." She looked at me. "When they hear a word, they understand the literal meaning. Slang's different. It never translates well."

"Why would your husband move away from you? Don't

all married people live together like Mom and Dad?" Kerr asked.

"They're supposed to. Sometimes, marriages just don't work out and couples get divorced," Mya said. She gave me an apologetic glance.

"It's okay. His leaving doesn't hurt as much as it used to. So much has happened since then. It was well over a year ago that he told me he was done. I just want my son back."

She frowned. "Isn't your son eight months old?"

"Yeah."

"What a dick."

"I don't understand," Drav said.

"She was pregnant when he told her he wanted a divorce."

Drav nodded slowly.

"Now, I understand. We will find him. You can have the divorce and remove your rings. It is a good plan."

I twisted the rings on my finger as his words hit a chord.

"I'm not sure how easy it will be to get a divorce now. Know any lawyers?" I asked Mya with a wry smile I didn't feel.

"I don't. But we'll worry about that after you find him and your son. For now, let's get this list put together."

I nodded and tried to focus on the items she mentioned, but my mind wandered.

What would I do if I found Lee and Caden? There were several options quietly waiting in the back of my mind. The most likely option was that I'd find nothing but empty houses. The idea of them being long dead shredded me on the inside. But I'd promised myself, if that were the case, I'd remove the rings and move on, focusing on keeping Lilly safe. Yet, there was another option that lurked in the dark, desperate recesses of my mind. To my shame, it was that I'd find both of them, and Lee would see the error he made, beg for my forgiveness, and want to take me back as if I were the one who'd walked away. I hated myself for even allowing that option to dwell in my mind. However, how could I not? The only way for Caden to be alive was for Lee to be alive. To hope for one meant I had to hope for both.

"What about animals?" she asked, pulling my attention back to the conversation.

"What do you mean?"

"Any chance there were chicken farms around where you were going? Eden said they had chickens in the bunker, so I think there might be some out there still. If we could find them, that would help a lot. We'd have eggs and fresh meat."

"I honestly don't know."

"We'll check the farms we pass," Drav said.

"That's a long list already. Unless you're talking a semi, which I can't drive, you might want a second truck with cages if you're serious about animals," I said.

"She's right." Mya gave Drav a pointed look. "Someone else should go with Cassie."

"Why? We know how to drive," Drav said.

"Yes, but you're more useful outside of the vehicle. Not inside of it."

"If we find animals, we will find another truck. Running

two vehicles draws more attention and is unnecessary without reason."

The idea of being out there on my own with over fifty fey unsettled me. I would have no understanding person to lean on when things got hard. And I knew they would. Being on my own sucked. The last several weeks proved that.

Rather than dwelling on the things I couldn't control, I focused on the things that I could.

"Whiteman needs the basics to keep people healthy and warm. Food in any form, hygiene products, and medical supplies for common, non-threatening injuries. Bedding and clothes are good, for now. Wood for the stoves in the tents, but that's not something we need to bring from far away.

"So pretty much everything we would find within what's left of the towns between here and Parsons. You wouldn't happen to have a map, would you?"

It took several minutes to round up the selection of maps the fey had found during previous hunting trips. We had enough to roughly piece together the area between Whiteman and Parsons.

"The core of Kansas City was bombed, so don't count on cutting over on thirty-five," Mya said. "It's better to stick to routes that don't go near the really big cities."

"Heading south on thirteen looks like the best bet," I said. Using my finger, I traced the road south. "Looks like Clinton might be our first stop then."

"We checked there and the outer homes had no food," Drav said.

Mya shrugged. "Whiteman was raiding the outskirts of

all the nearby towns before we got here. But they tended to leave the interiors alone. Look at Warrensburg. You guys are still finding stuff there."

"Not so much food anymore. But yes, we will look at Clinton again," he said.

"Okay," I said. "After Clinton, we'll cut over on eighteen to Butler. Hopefully, one of those places will have a clinic or something. Then forty-nine down to Nevada and down to Fort Scott." I stared at the map and sighed. If we checked every town between Tolerance and Parsons, it would take a week to get there.

Mya seemed to read my mind.

"It might be better to save a few towns for the way back. You don't want a full truck before you even get to Parsons."

"Right."

We talked for another hour, plotting the route and the possibilities. In the end, Mya and I decided I would play everything by ear regarding where and when to stop to look for supplies.

"Are you sure I'm the best person to put in charge?" I asked her.

"You'll know what looks normal in town and what looks off. You can also read signs and know the most likely places to find the supplies needed. The fey will get you where you need to go. Trust them to keep you safe. They will. They know the infecteds' tricks and can spot traps. They're good at what they do."

"What do you think we're looking at for a timeline if we stop at the towns I mentioned?" I asked, studying the map.

"Three or four days to get to Parsons. Three to four days to get back."

I exhaled heavily and rubbed my face. A week away from Lilly was a lot.

"Don't think about what could or should be done. Commit and stick to what you decide. Stay in the moment and live it. That's all any of us can do. Doubt, hesitation, guilt...it's all just a distraction we can't afford. Do you understand?"

Mya may have looked younger, but her wisdom made her feel years older than me.

The back door burst open, and Lilly came racing in.

"I have a friend," she said, launching herself into my arms.

I caught her and hugged her tightly, unable to believe the joy I'd glimpsed on her face.

"You do?" I said. "Who is your friend?"

"His name is Timmy. Byllo is his new Daddy, and he said I can play with Timmy tomorrow." She pulled back to look me in the eye. "Timmy plays with toys," she said in sudden seriousness. "But they're quiet ones, and Byllo says they are safe."

A week away from her would feel like forever. But in my heart, I knew she'd be safer here than with me.

"I'm so excited you made a friend," I said.

"You'll get to meet him tonight. Miss Julie invited him over for dinner. A lot of people are coming. Can I go back over and play with Timmy until it's time to eat?"

I looked at Julie who was still standing beside the door.

"I told her she needed to ask you."

"It's all right with me."

She opened the door, and Lilly slid off my lap to run to the big man standing just outside.

"This is Shax," Julie said. "He'll walk her back to Byllo and Timmy so that I can start cooking."

I nodded to the fey, vaguely recalling him from the morning journey to Tolerance. Again, the shifting reality of my life hit me. So much was happening so fast. And more would happen over the next several days. The stress I'd felt last night had melted into a numb state of "go with the flow." Mya was right about my need to decide and commit. There wasn't going to be time for anything else.

CHAPTER SEVEN

I SLIPPED OUT THE BACKDOOR AND TOOK A DEEP BREATH OF the cold night air. The stifling temperature of Julie's kitchen had made me sweat. Something I'd been sure I'd never do again.

Spotting a snow-free chair on the patio, I took a seat, ready to let myself cool off and enjoy the fresh air. The sun hung low in the sky but still had an hour before it set.

"It's too cold out here for you, Cassie," a familiar voice said.

I turned my head toward the trees. It took a moment to see Kerr standing there so still.

"It was too hot in the kitchen. I needed to escape outside for a minute."

He walked over to me and reached for my face. The gentle press of the back of his hand to my forehead surprised me.

"You are warm."

I smiled slightly. It was something I would say to Lilly if she would have complained about not feeling well.

"It will pass. I've never seen so much food cooked at once. It makes the kitchen too hot."

Kerr removed his hand then sat in the chair next to mine. He barely fit.

"Can I ask you questions, Cassie? Mya says it's not okay to ask questions without permission."

"You guys really listen to Mya, don't you?"

"She's human and knows your rules. She also keeps us safe. She is wise."

"Yeah, she is. Yes, you may ask me questions."

"Why do some couples not work out?"

I don't know what I'd expected him to ask, but it wasn't that.

"Well, I guess it's because some people don't take time to know each other first."

"Your husband did not know you?"

"He knew the common things, like what I liked to eat and what I liked to do, but neither of us took time to find out what motivates each other. He was very motivated by money. Family and quality time together motivated me."

Kerr studied me for a moment.

"Family still motivates you."

"It does. But safety is a bigger motivator right now. I want Lilly and me to be able to sleep through the night again. And maybe even find a way to be happy. I think feeling safe is something that probably motivates everyone lately."

Kerr looked away for a second.

"You don't feel safe here?"

I realized he was looking at the distant wall. As I watched, light shot into the sky from a set of headlights. One by one, cars within the wall began to light up the sky and the occasional snowflake drifting down.

"That's beautiful," I said softly before meeting his intense gaze. "I feel safer here. But, I also feel more scared."

He frowned slightly.

"It's hard to explain. Life's been bad for so long, feeling safe just reminds me that I still have a lot to lose. And I'm not sure I can deal with any additional loss. It feels like just one more thing will break me. I'm trying to hold it all together, but…"

I sighed and looked at the sky. With effort, I pulled back the emotions that were trying to drag me down into the ever-waiting pit of depression opened by those damn earthquakes.

"Are you ever afraid when you go outside the wall?" I asked.

"No. There is nothing out there for me to fear. The infected are slow and stupid. The hellhounds are dangerous alone, but I am never alone. However, I fear returning to Tolerance."

I pulled my attention from the sky to look at him.

"Why?"

"Out there, it is easy to forget I have no reason to return here."

I wasn't sure what to say. The desire to find a woman of their own was a common theme among the fey. I wasn't that woman, though. Never again. Not for a human or a fey.

"I hope you find someone, Kerr." I moved to stand, but he stopped me with another question.

"What was he like? Your husband."

"Lee?" At his nod, I contemplated the man I'd married versus the man who told me he wanted a divorce.

"He was handsome and sweet in the beginning. He brought me things, small gifts to show me he appreciated me. But the gifts didn't really mean anything. They were just displays of his affection for things rather than for me. I didn't know that then.

"We were good together at first. We went places and had fun. It wasn't until after we had Lilly that things started to change. He only wanted to go on vacations and do things that didn't include Lilly. I was fine with short getaways but started to feel like I was being made to choose between the two of them. He was never content to stay home and spend time together as a family. It was weird.

"I could see he loved Lilly but not enough to be content with a simple life. He wanted me to go back to work fulltime even though, financially, we were okay with me being a stay-at-home mom. We argued a lot about that before I ended up giving in.

"At some point, I started realizing that things were really broken. I didn't realize how broken until I got pregnant with Caden. It was unplanned. I thought Lee would be excited when I told him, but he was completely the opposite.

"Only a few weeks after that, he told me he wanted a divorce."

I thought of Lee. Of how he'd been with Lilly and how he'd been as a person.

"He loved having fun. He was always planning the next adventure. He took Lilly to ballgames and shows. For four, she'd seen and done a lot before the earthquakes."

I stopped talking and looked at Kerr.

"He loves his kids. And he used to love me. But he wasn't ready to give up his freedom so he could raise a family."

"I don't understand divorce," Kerr said, sounding almost angry. "I understand the word and what the meaning is, but the concept doesn't make sense. If a male finds a woman who is willing to love him, why would he ever want to leave?"

I smiled at Kerr.

"I wish more men thought like you."

His gaze pinned me, and the moment of silence grew too serious. I quickly stood.

"I better get back inside. I'll see you at dinner, yes?"

"I will be there."

Mya grinned at me from her position near the stove when I went back inside.

"What were you and Kerr talking about?" she asked.

"Divorce. He said he didn't understand the concept of it. Why a man would leave a woman who loves him. The fey really have no clue, do they?"

"They understand humans well enough," she said. "They just don't understand why we do the stupid things we do."

"Truer words were never spoken," Julie said. "Relationships tend to really boggle them. Just wait until they start asking to see your pussy."

My mouth dropped open.

"Mom!" Mya gave her mother a censuring look, and Julie laughed hard.

"They won't really ask that. Will they?" I asked.

"Oh, they will," Julie said.

"I hope not," Mya said. "I've told them repeatedly they can't use that word." She looked up at her mom, a mischievous grin on her face. "You know what Eden told me? Ghua learned the word vagina. It's his new favorite word."

Julie chuckled. "Won't be long before they all start using it."

"You're making me even more nervous about this trip," I said.

Mya waved her hand.

"You don't have to worry about them. They'll ask questions and make you turn three shades of red and probably make you want to hide in the corner, but that's the worst of it. They're very sweet and loyal, and they care."

I hung up my jacket and hoped she was right.

Just a few minutes before dark, the first of the guests showed up. Eden opened the door after a brief knock and held up a box of wine.

"Check out what Ghua found on his last run into Warrensburg. He wasn't sure what it was but knew human children like juice." She pointed toward the dark purple liquid shown on the box.

"They do," he said from behind her. "I did not know there was adult juice, too."

"And, now you know," Eden said, grinning.

Julie took the box and poured us all a glass of wine. I took a tentative sip and exhaled slowly. Another forever ago item I thought I'd never taste again.

Eden caught my content expression and winked at me.

"Moving to Tolerance has its perks."

"Yes," Ghua said. "You get to live with me."

Eden leaned back against him and turned her head for a kiss.

The pair had barely settled into their chairs when another knock sounded at the door. Several young women came in and were introduced to me as the survivors of the RV that Mya's group had found on their way to Whiteman. I recalled the group and the story of the fey finding them in the nick of time. Thirteen more survivors to bolster Whiteman's human numbers. Although, not all of them had decided to stay at Whiteman when the fey moved to Tolerance.

"I'm Hannah," the blonde said with a smile. "And this is Emily."

"Nice to finally meet you," I said. "I've had the pleasure of meeting Mary and James, and they told me a lot about your time outside the fence."

Emily shuddered and looked down. A very normal reaction for anyone thinking of life outside the protection of Whiteman or Tolerance.

"How are they?" Hannah asked. "Are Connor and Caleb staying out of trouble?"

"They must be because I haven't seen them."

Before long, the room was full of people, including Nancy, a wheelchair bound woman with a level of tenacity and courage I envied greatly. Her daughter, Brenna, and son, Zachy, didn't say much as they sat back and watched the others interact.

I couldn't believe how many survivors had already moved to Tolerance. I hadn't really paid attention at the time the fey had left. I'd only been relieved that the intimidating creatures were gone. However, as a few of the fey came in, I was starting to understand my mistake. No one here feared the fey. The women laughed and talked openly, getting along with each and every dark-skinned man.

The final group to join the dinner party included my daughter and two other children. A woman, not much older than me, held a little girl, no more than two, in her arms. Seeing a child younger than Lilly gave me a cautious boost of hope of finding Caden alive.

Lilly hung back with a little boy and another large, dark-skinned fey. Before I could call Lilly's name, the woman approached me.

"You must be Cassie," she said with a welcoming smile. "I'm Jessie, and this is my daughter Savannah. We're so glad you're here. Another playmate is just what we needed to keep these two busy."

She turned and looked back at the fey and boy.

"I'm Timmy," the boy said realizing he had our attention. "This is my new dad, Byllo. He's strong and fast."

Byllo placed a gentle hand on the boy's head.

"It's nice to meet you," I said, looking at him, then Jessie. "I'm relieved that Lilly has someone her age."

Jessie nodded in understanding.

"We'll help keep her distracted," she said quietly.

Before anymore could be said, Julie called for everyone's attention.

"Let's eat!"

JULIE and I worked side-by-side in the kitchen, cleaning up the remains of dinner while Lilly checked out the toys in the bedroom. The last guest had left not long ago, and it felt good to be in a less crowded space.

"What did you think of your first dinner here?" she asked, handing me the next pot to dry.

"It was interesting." I hesitated to say what was really on my mind then decided life was too short and went for it. "I thought you said hooking up wasn't required."

She chuckled.

"It's not, but it seems to happen eventually. The fey are very interested in women."

"Yeah, I know that. But it seems like it's a little bit pushed."

"What do you mean?"

"Well, take Hannah for example. Shax seems very interested in her. He kept trying to talk her into going for a walk with him when she obviously didn't want to. And, Mya was encouraging Hannah to change her mind even after Hannah's repeated and polite declines."

I put the pot aside and took the next one from Julie.

"Mya wants the fey to be happy," Julie said. "My

daughter sees them all as brothers. Of course, she's going to try to set them up. Just like she tries to set up Ryan. Nothing seems to stick, though. She knows that whatever happens will happen on its own, without her meddling, but she can't seem to help herself. She doesn't mean any harm by it."

I dried the next few dishes in contemplative silence. Mya might not mean harm by it, but her gentle prods had made me uncomfortable. How long until she set her sights on me? I recalled her grin when I'd come in from talking to Kerr and knew it wouldn't be too long.

"Have any of the fey ever gotten angry for being told no?" I asked.

"No. And let me tell you, they've been told no plenty. Some not so nicely. Honestly, they are happy just to have a girl talking to them. It's kind of sad, really. I understand why Mya tries so hard. I'm not going to lie. I have hopes that they will all find their happiness, too."

Given what the fey did for us humans, I could understand why she felt that way. I just didn't want to be the other half of any pairing.

"I think Kerr's interested in me."

"I think you're right. Is that a bad thing?" She glanced at me, and I knew she was trying to gauge my reaction.

"For him, yes. I'm not looking for a man to complicate my life again. I just want to feel safe and not used for a while."

"That makes sense. Tell Kerr that when you run into him next. It's kinder to be upfront with what you're feeling rather than let him get his hopes up. The fey understand they aren't every girl's dream, and they respect that, even in rejection."

Her words made me feel small and narrow-minded. Rather than trying to defend my choices, I kept quiet and hurried through the rest of the dishes.

When we finished, I said goodnight and went upstairs. I found Lilly sitting on the edge of her twin bed, already wearing the pajamas I'd put out for her.

"Hey, Lilly-bean. I thought I'd find you playing with the toys."

She shook her head.

"It's too quiet and dark out."

"I understand." I sat beside her and hugged her to my side. "Did you have fun today?"

"Yes. A lot. Timmy was loud, and Byllo didn't tell him to be quiet. And Savvy cried lots."

"What about with Miss Julie? Did you like spending time with her?"

"Yes. She's nice." Lilly rubbed her head against me. "Are you going to find Daddy and Caden?"

"I'm going to try."

"I'll miss you."

"I'm going to miss you, too. So much."

She pulled away to crawl under the comforter.

"I'm going to go change and brush my teeth. Will you be okay?"

She nodded.

I left the room with the pajamas Julie had loaned me and hurried through getting ready for bed. When I stepped out of the bathroom in a simple long t-shirt, it felt weird without all the layers.

Lilly watched me turn off the light and moved over so I could slide in next to her. Lying in the twin bed with Lilly was cozy. But, we both held still in the dark. I strained to hear anything beyond the sounds of our breathing and the swish of the washing machine downstairs. Several heartbeats passed before Lilly turned her head toward me.

"I don't hear anything, Mommy."

"Me neither. It's nice, isn't it?"

"No. It's scary."

"Only because we aren't used to it. Nothing has ever gotten through the wall here. Miss Julie told me."

She looked toward the window then quickly slipped out of bed. I watched her pull back the curtain and stare outside for a moment.

"He won't let anything get us," she said, dropping the curtain back into place.

She climbed over me and nestled in under the blankets once more.

"He?"

"Yeah. The man outside. The one who gave me the bead."

"Kerr?"

I got out of bed and went to the window. Across the street, a fey stood on the shoveled sidewalk. From this distance, I couldn't tell who it was in the dim light.

"How do you know it's him?" I asked.

"Because it is."

The figure turned from his study of the yards around us and looked up at the window. In that moment, I knew Lilly was right. I still couldn't clearly see his face, but something in the way he held himself gave it away.

It was Kerr standing out there. But why?

I let the curtain drop back in place and chewed my lip for a moment while mentally replaying my conversation with Julie. He needed to know I wasn't interested. Besides, having him lurk outside the house was creepy.

"Stay here," I said to Lilly.

I ran into Julie in the hall just as she was coming upstairs.

"Everything okay?"

"Kerr's outside. I need to talk to him like you said."

"It might be for the best," she said with a nod. "I'll sit with Lilly until you get back. Just so she's not afraid on her first night here."

"Thank you, Julie. For everything."

"Oh, it's no problem."

I jogged down the stairs and quickly tossed on my coat and shoes. My toes curled at the no-sock, direct contact. I didn't want to go back upstairs, though. If I did, I might not come back down.

A cold swirl of air encased my legs as I opened the door and stepped outside.

Kerr saw me and jogged across the street. I stepped away from the front door to meet him on the sidewalk.

"Why are you out here?" His gaze swept over me, lingering on my bare legs.

Why was I wishing I'd shaved? No one shaved their legs

anymore. There wasn't any point. Yet, under his close scrutiny, I was beginning to think there might be.

"I was going to ask you the same thing. Why are you standing outside, Kerr?"

"You wanted to feel safe again."

I looked down the street, noticing other shadows moving.

"You're not the only one out here."

"No. The others are guarding the walls."

"And you're guarding me?"

"Yes. It's too cold for you out here. Go back inside. You're safe."

I shivered but didn't turn around.

"Kerr, if you're doing this because you want me to hook up with you, I don't want you to get your hopes up. My priorities are keeping my kids safe and healthy. That's it." I shook my head. "I'm just not able to do more than that."

"I know. You still wear his rings."

He stepped closer, crowding into my personal space. His arms closed around me. This time, when he lifted me, his hands were on the bare skin of my legs. Heat radiated off of him. I shivered and looked up into his eyes.

"After we find him, you can remove your rings and be free to choose again."

His fingers caressed my skin a moment before he set me down again. When he leaned forward, I retreated a step, eyes wide and heart hammering. He followed, reaching around me. I stepped back again, an odd mixture of fear and excitement tumbling together in my belly.

"We will speak more tomorrow," he said.

The door clicked open behind me. It was only then that I realized he'd placed me on the stoop.

"Sleep well, and know you are safe."

He gently guided me inside then closed the door.

I stood there and stared blankly at the floor before quickly shedding the coat and shoes and bolting upstairs.

"How did it go?" Julie asked when I entered the bedroom.

"I think I made it worse."

"Yeah, not wearing pants probably gave him mixed signals."

I swore under my breath as she grinned and left the room. I couldn't help but wonder what in the hell I'd say to Kerr tomorrow.

CHAPTER EIGHT

I woke up alone. For one terrifying moment, I thought someone had taken Lilly away from me, and I sat up in a rush. Over the thundering of my heart, I heard her childish voice coming from down the hall.

Sliding from bed, I followed the sound. Lilly was standing still in front of the bathroom mirror, watching as Julie braided her hair.

Julie looked up and smiled.

"Good morning. Did you sleep well?"

"Very. The best night's sleep in a long time. What time did Lilly get up?"

"Just a bit ago."

"I had pancakes, Mommy."

"There are still some on the table for you," Julie said. "I thought we'd let you sleep in."

"Thank you."

"Miss Julie said I can spend today with her and Timmy if it's okay with you. Can I, Mommy? Please?"

I met my daughter's eyes in the mirror.

"All right. While you play, I'll explore a bit. How about I check in at—

"Dinner?" Julie suggested.

Yesterday had been a great test run for Lilly. She'd had fun and had done just fine without me around. It made sense to try for a longer period today. After all, she and I only had another day or two together before I had to leave for almost a week.

"You're okay spending the day with Miss Julie?" I asked.

"Yep."

"Have fun and be a good girl, okay?"

"I will, Mommy. I love you."

I kissed the top of her head and quietly went back to the bedroom.

Dressing in the same clothes as the day before, I considered what to do with myself for the day. One of the girls last night had mentioned a shed they used to store all the extra supplies. Perhaps I could check that out and compare what I found to the list of what was needed.

Content with the start of my plans, I went downstairs.

Julie and Lilly were already bundling up by the door.

"It snowed last night, Mommy," Lilly said with a smile. "We're going to make angels."

"That sounds really fun."

"While you're out exploring, you might want to look at the unclaimed houses. You can pick which one you'd like to call your own," Julie said. "That way, we'll have it all cleaned out and painted for you when you return."

"Sure. I'll take a look."

Lilly waved goodbye, and I was left alone in Julie's kitchen. I helped myself to a few pancakes with syrup and considered having my own home again. The prospect was scary. Mostly it was just the idea of being alone. I liked the idea of having heat and walls again, though.

But first, I had to leave. I took a bite of pancake and wondered what I'd need for the trip. The hunting party already out was due back tomorrow, so I needed to start packing enough food to last a week. I hurried through my pancakes and glass of milk, which was a pleasant treat, and bundled up to find the supply shed.

This time when I saw Kerr standing in the back yard, waiting for me, I didn't mind.

"Hey, Kerr. Can you show me where the supply shed is?"

"Good morning, Cassie."

The way he said the greeting, like he'd just rolled over in bed, made my insides shiver. I studied him for a moment, noting he'd changed clothes from the night before and how the dark jacket he now wore pulled snugly across his chest with his arms crossed. My mouth went a little dry at the display.

"Hey. Yah. Good morning."

I looked away before I started to blush. Kerr was sure built to last. All of the fey were. I rubbed my small arms and tried not to think how weak I was in comparison.

"Did you eat breakfast already?" he asked.

"I just finished some pancakes Julie left for me. About the storage shed? I'm hoping that I can pack up some supplies for tomorrow so I can spend some time with Lilly later."

"You will not need supplies. Everything you need, we will gather along the way."

"Oh." He'd just shot my plans for the day. I wondered what I was supposed to do next and remembered Julie's suggestion.

"Julie thought I should look at the houses. Do you know which ones aren't taken?"

"Yes. I will show you."

He led the way around to the front of the house. Together, we walked along the shoveled sidewalk.

"Who takes care of all the snow?" I asked.

"We do. Those of us who guard the walls at night. I cleared these since I was here last night."

"About that. You really don't need to stand outside Julie's house all night. I appreciate the gesture, but I know it's safe here."

"Do you?"

His quiet question gave me pause. I looked around at the yards and realized my gaze still searched for infected shambling around in the shadows. As much as I wanted to feel safe in Tolerance, I couldn't let myself relax. I didn't see that being a bad thing, though. People who let their guard down died.

"So, how do you know which houses are unclaimed?" I asked, changing the subject.

"The mailboxes," he said. "The ones with the flags up are unclaimed."

We didn't pass many with the flags up.

"I know where Mya and Drav live and, obviously, Julie. But where do the other humans live?"

"They all have houses, here, in the center. Some of them share houses. They feel safer together."

"What about you guys? Do you share houses?"

"No. Many of us have claimed our own houses."

"Fey don't like living with each other?" I asked.

"We all hope to find our own females and have made our houses ready."

I looked at the homes around me. They all looked very similar which was normal for subdivisions. Nothing stood out to signal which houses were ready for a fey insta-family.

"What do you mean by ready?"

"I will show you."

I followed him down the block to a quaint stone and wood home done in greys and blues. He walked up to the front door and opened it.

"Whose house is this?"

"This is my home."

I stepped inside. There wasn't much to the modest living room. A sofa and a chair and a television. The walls were bare of any pictures, and the room smelled faintly of fresh paint.

Kerr pulled off his leather boots and went to the kitchen. I kicked off my shoes and followed.

One by one, he opened the cupboards. Food filled each

storage space. Boxes and boxes of cheesy noodle dinners and cans of chicken and tuna. One cupboard had two shelves full of vegetables as well.

I'd seen Whiteman's supply room in the hangar and knew the fey had been giving plenty to the survivors there as well. But, the sheer amount of what they had to be collecting stunned me.

"That's a lot of food," I said.

"Humans feel safer when there is plenty to eat."

He closed the doors then went in the direction of the laundry room. He opened the storage closet to show me little stacks of towels and several sets of feminine clothes. I reached out and looked at the sizes. They were all within the range of what I wore.

I stepped back, and he closed the cupboard and studied me.

"How long have you been collecting things?" I asked.

"Since we moved to Tolerance."

That wasn't long after they arrived at Whiteman. A week maybe two. That meant he had been collecting things for close to a month. The food made sense. The clothes, though? All about the same size?

"Were you collecting the clothes for a particular person?" I asked the question even though I really didn't want to hear the answer.

"Yes."

The way he looked at me made it clear who he hoped would move in with him.

"Kerr, I meant what I said last night. I can't think about a new relationship right now."

"I understand. I can think of nothing else, though."

My stomach did an odd swan-dive to my toes at the heat in his gaze. He didn't make a move to touch me or say anything more. However, I still felt the need to run.

"I think I should get going." I hated that I was retreating but didn't know what else to do. Reaching out and touching him sure wasn't an option, no matter how much my fingers twitched to do just that.

"Where will you go?" he asked.

He had me there. There wasn't anywhere to go in Tolerance. And nothing to keep me busy.

"Are Merdon and Thallirin still here?" I asked hopefully.

"No. They left this morning. Merdon's leg is healing well."

Damn.

"Fine. You're right. There's nowhere to go. And, I honestly have no idea what I'm supposed to do with myself. You're saying there's nothing to pack. And Julie wants to keep Lilly to herself today, as a test run, to make sure Lilly won't miss me too much while I'm gone."

He considered me for a moment.

"Would you like to watch a movie?" he asked.

"I don't think that's a good idea. I don't want to give you the impression that I'm caving in. I don't want a man in my life, Kerr. The last one caused me nothing but heartache."

"He was human. I am fey and will cause you no heartache."

"How can you say that? You don't even know me or what would break my heart."

"I know what motivates you. You said that was the most important thing."

It would have been easy to get annoyed with him if he were being sarcastic. Instead, his tone and his expression conveyed his sincerity and his confusion. He didn't just want me. He wanted to be what I needed. It was so sweet, and I felt a moment of pity for him.

"You'd be far better off going after one of the single girls here. Someone like Hannah, who doesn't have kids. I'm a complex package, Kerr. You don't want that."

"I know what I want. I've known since the moment I saw you arguing with Matt Davis the day after we arrived. You did not back down, and you walked away angry. Your red hair was tied back in a ponytail."

He reached out and gently touched my hair before dropping his hand. My insides did a funny dance that I hadn't felt for years.

"Your determination and anger caught my attention. The way you spoke to the other humans and tried to help even when you were so angry kept my attention."

"Most men would be turned off by displays of anger."

"I am not most men."

No, he wasn't. And that was part of the problem.

"You're putting me in a tough position, Kerr. I'm telling you no, and you keep telling me yes. What am I supposed to do with that?"

"Be patient. Focus on finding your son and husband.

Trust that I will keep you safe. Trust that I will help you remove that ring."

I couldn't believe his level of tenacity. There was no arguing with his complete certainty that he wanted me. Retreat was definitely the wisest course.

"Thank you for showing me your home. I think I'd like to spend the rest of today with Lilly."

I walked out the door and didn't look back.

It took a while, but I found Julie and Lilly by following the sound of childish laughter. They were in the backyard of another house along with Jessie, Timmy, and Savvy.

"Hey guys," I called. "Do you have room for one more?" The children stopped moving their arms and legs to look up at me from their positions in the snow. Several fey were standing further away, watching their antics.

Julie smiled and stood from her seat on the patio furniture.

"We weren't expecting to see you until after dinner," she said, walking toward me.

"I know. Turns out there isn't so much to do here. I thought I'd come hang out with you and Lilly." I waved at Lilly.

"See if you can teach Byllo how to make a snow angel," Julie called to the children.

Lilly and Timmy squealed and jumped up to get the big man who stood nearby. When Julie looked at me again, I could tell by the slight change in her expression that something was wrong. She kept her smile in place as she hooked her arm through mine and led me toward the front of the house.

"Why do I feel like I'm in trouble?" I asked.

Julie chuckled.

"Because you have a lot of experience with it?"

She stopped walking and faced me.

"I understand you want to spend time with Lilly, but she's a smart kid. She'll know something is going on if you start clinging to her just before you need to leave."

She was right. But, selfishly, I didn't care. If this was the last day I had with Lilly, I wanted to pack it full of memories.

Julie set her hand on my arm.

"You're not going to die out there, Cassie. And you need to act like you believe that, or you're going to leave behind a terrified little girl."

Her words speared me. I couldn't do that to Lilly. Yet, a rational part of me also argued it was unfair to rob her of my time if there was only a little left.

"How do you know I'm not going to die? It's dangerous."

Julie patted my arm and gave me a small smile.

"I have a son and husband. Do you know where they are? Out there with the fey, helping with a scavenging hunt. And, I'm not the slightest bit worried. Do you know why? Because I've seen what these men can do. I know they will keep my husband and my son safe. You need to trust. You need to have faith. That's the only way Lilly will ever have faith that you're going to come back."

"So I'm supposed to act like everything's okay?"

"No. You're supposed to believe everything is going to be

okay. Because it will be. Now, go and have some fun. Lilly's safe and enjoying herself."

I looked around at the snow-covered yards.

"What exactly am I supposed to do for fun?"

"You'll figure something out."

She winked at me and walked around back.

Once more, I found myself wandering the sidewalks of Tolerance. It wasn't that big of a space, and I was starting to become familiar with the houses. I wasn't alone in my wanderings. Many of the fey walked around, likewise bored it seemed. Anytime I met up with one, he would smile and nod at me. I could see the hope in their eyes now. So much like Kerr. Was I making the wrong choice living here? Yes, it was physically safer, but was I setting them all up for hurt and rejection?

I walked back to Julie's house and let myself in. I browsed her movie selection and plugged in a comedy.

From the couch, I stared at the screen. I tried really hard to focus on the characters and let them take me away. However, sometimes escape from reality wasn't so easy.

Before the movie ended, I heard the back door open. I stood quickly, relieved that someone could help distract me from my boredom. I should have known it wouldn't be the person I'd hoped for.

Kerr met my gaze the moment I stepped through the kitchen arch.

"I would like to show you something," he said.

I hesitated, debating if I should use the movie as an excuse to claim I was busy. There was every chance he'd want to join me, though, given he'd asked if I wanted to watch a movie with him only a few hours ago.

"Okay. What do you want to show me?"

"You will need your shoes and warm clothes."

He watched me closely as I bundled up then held the door for me when I stepped outside.

Before I knew what he intended, he picked me up and raced toward the wall. I squealed when he jumped and wrapped my arms around his neck to hold on tightly. I didn't miss the way his fingers lightly petted my leg in return.

Instead of going all the way over, he landed directly on top of the wall, and I looked down at the collection of jammed-together junk and cars on which he stood.

"What are you doing?" I asked.

"Showing you why I keep telling you yes."

I removed my hold around his neck.

"I know why you want me to say yes. You've already told me all fey want a woman of their own. I get it. I just don't want to be that woman for anyone."

"It isn't just about what I want. It's about what you need."

My mouth dropped open at that presumptuous statement, but he didn't give me a chance to reply.

He started moving again, jogging along the top of the wall. We passed several fey on the ground. They barely noted his passing with a wave before continuing their patrol.

Not far from where we started, Kerr stopped and set me on my feet.

The wind buffeted me, and I shivered. Kerr moved closer, standing directly behind me. I jumped when he wrapped an arm around my waist. With his other hand, he pointed. I tried to ignore the heat of his front pressed against my back and followed the direction he indicated.

Nancy, the woman in the wheelchair who I'd met the night before, sat on the back patio of a house not far from where we stood. Molev stood near her, speaking in low tones. I could hear the rumble of his voice but not his words.

Even from this distance, I could see the misery in the woman's gaze.

"What's going on?" I asked.

"Molev is speaking to Nancy. Her husband was killed by raiders south of here. Her daughter was raped. They both hold anger inside. Neither wants a man in her life. Molev is telling Nancy that having no one in her life will lead to a lonely existence. It is something we fey know well. I have lived thousands of lives. Each lonelier than the one before. It is not something any fey would want for a female."

"What does that mean? Is he forcing her to hook up with someone?"

"No. He is telling her that allowing someone in her life will show her daughter that it is safe to do the same. This way, her daughter will not know the same lonely existence as her mother."

The gentle press of Kerr's arm around my middle kept me from turning and trying to punch him.

"Is this you trying to talk me into hooking up? I told you no, dammit."

"Not hooking up. Having a friend." His calm, sad words settled me a little. "In this world, children grow old, and people die. Who will you have when Lilly is no longer a child?"

"And you want that someone to be you?"

"I would like that. But, if you would prefer someone else, that is okay too. Just don't choose to be alone forever. That is not living. Only existing."

His words hit home. I'd experienced the loneliness he spoke of, and I didn't want to go back. Yet, I didn't want to dive into the wrong relationship just so I wouldn't be alone. Both options had their own levels of hell.

I took a step away from him and turned to look up into his eyes.

"What exactly do you want from me?"

CHAPTER NINE

"YOUR COMPANY," KERR SAID.

"I don't think that's what you really want, but fine. For today, you can have my company. So, what do you want to do?"

I waited for him to reach for me. To make some kind of pass. Instead, he looked off into the distance and idly scratched the tip of one elongated ear. I doubted I'd ever get used to that.

"Do you like to play games?" he asked finally. "Some of the others are playing games with juice boxes tonight. We are invited."

"Sure. Games are fine. What about till then?"

The pass I expected never came.

"Do you know how to read?" he asked.

"Of course."

"Will you teach me?"

He had my attention.

"I can try, but I can't make any promises. I'm no teacher."

"You're not a doctor, either, but you do that very well."

On top of the wall in the wind and cold, something shifted inside of me. A sense of worth that had long ago been buried.

"Thank you, Kerr. That was a really nice thing to say."

"Can I carry you home? I have books I want to read."

"Sure."

He picked me up and jogged back the way he'd come before jumping down from the wall. We were back at his house in seconds this time.

"Before you can read your books, you'll need to learn the alphabet. Do you have pen and paper?"

We spent the next hour going over the ABCs. I taught him the song while making lunch and wrote down capital and lowercase letters while he washed the dishes. He listened attentively as I went over each sound, and I wished Lilly was there. This was all stuff I should have started teaching her, but with the new baby and then the zombie apocalypse, spending time on non-survival things just kind of stopped mattering.

Kerr learned quickly but not instantly like he did with spoken words. By the time four o'clock rolled around, he could identify each letter in its case and make all the sounds without error.

"Let's work on your name next," I said.

"No. It is time to go to Hannah and Emily's house for games. Thank you for teaching me letters."

He helped with my jacket and walked beside me as we made our way to Hannah's house. The fey idling in the yards outside nodded as we passed.

"Is it boring living here?" I asked Kerr.

"No. It's different. But much like our lives before. Periods of idle time and periods of training and leaving for supplies."

I'd heard the story of their origin but wasn't quite sure if I believed it. Fey cursed by their own people because of the crystals that existed in the cave system they'd found.

"Is it true that you used to live underground?" I asked.

"Yes, in caverns beneath the surface."

"And you're saying that living up here is the same as what it was down there?"

"Similar, but not the same. We had a wall of stone that protected us from the hellhounds, and there were no infected below."

Trapped in the dark with nothing but hellhounds outside of their wall sounded horrific. That he thought this was similar to how he'd lived in the caverns was just sad. I hated how humans had to live now. I couldn't imagine lifetimes of hiding in fear behind walls.

"And you really couldn't die down there?"

"Our lives ended many times, but we were always reborn."

He gestured to a house that had the front door open. A low murmur of voices drifted out as we walked up the path.

"Cassie, I'm so glad Kerr talked you into coming," Hannah said the moment I stepped in the door. "These get-togethers are more fun with bigger groups, and Mya and Eden never want in."

Given the current state of the living room, I understood why. It was obvious just what kind of party Hannah and Emily were having. The furniture had been pushed back and a table setup in the middle of the space. There were no chairs. Just red plastic cups and a pyramid of six wine boxes. Either Kerr had misunderstood what the girls meant when they'd suggested a game night, or he was completely clueless about drinking games.

Kerr closed the door behind us before I could figure out a way to bow out.

"Have you played quarters before?" Emily asked as Hannah filled the cups on the table.

"No," Shax, Kerr, and the other fey in the room said.

I'd played but knew that rules were often different from party to party.

"The rules are simple," Emily said. "All you need to do is get the quarter in the center cup by bouncing it off the table. If you get the quarter in the cup, everyone else gets to drink their juice."

I wanted to groan. They were playing to get drunk. I glanced at Kerr. Seeing a fey drunk was not anywhere on my list of entertaining things to do.

"You're not able to drink your juice unless I can get a quarter in the cup?" Shax asked.

"Do not worry," Kerr said, setting a hand on my shoulder. "I will get the quarter in the cup so you may drink."

"Oh, that's okay. I'm really not that thirsty."

Hannah picked up the quarter and demonstrated how to bounce it off the table. She hit the center cup, but didn't make it in.

"And when you miss, you have to drink," Hannah said. "How much you drink is up to you."

"Good," Kerr said. He lowered his head so his lips were almost touching my ear. "You can miss on purpose if you are thirsty." A shiver raced up my spine at the whispered words.

Kerr guided me closer to the table, and we both took our places. Shax took the quarter from Hannah and winked at her. The quarter bounced off the table and neatly into the center cup.

Kerr helpfully handed me my cup when I hesitated.

"You guys know that I leave tomorrow, right?" I asked, looking at Hannah and Emily.

"That's exactly why we thought this was the best game for tonight," Hannah said.

I took a cautious sip of wine and wondered how long until dinner time. Kerr picked up his cup and took a huge gulp.

"This is good," he said. "Adult juice is different from the other juice."

Hannah grinned widely.

"It's fermented," I said. "Alcohol."

"Aw! We weren't going to tell them." Emily made a pouty face.

I looked at the brunette and shrugged. Just what had she hoped would happen by not telling them?

"It is good," another fey said.

"Thanks for getting it for us, Shax and Tor," Hannah said.

"Did they get these from the supply shed?" I asked.

"Yep." Hannah grinned. "They got one for each of us."

Emily took the quarter and bounced it off the table, sinking it into the center cup. I took another small sip and watched the fey take huge gulps. This couldn't be good.

We'd only made it around the table once when someone knocked on the door.

"Come in," Hannah called, picking up the quarter for her next turn.

"Party pooper police," Eden said, opening the door. "Surrender your juice boxes."

"Aw, come on." Emily made good on another pouty face as Eden and Mya walked in.

"Were you honestly going to drink six boxes of wine tonight?" Mya asked, looking at Emily.

"Nope, but they might have."

I glanced at the three fey, thinking Emily was probably right. The fey liked the wine a bit too much.

Mya shook her head and sighed.

"I'm turning this into a girl's night, guys. Sorry, Kerr, Shax, and Tor, but you gotta go."

"Will you walk me out, Hannah?" Shax asked. His hopeful expression when he looked at her made me uncomfortable and brought back Kerr's words about their lonely lifetimes.

Hannah smiled at Shax kindly and patted his arm.

"I think I'll stick around to hear what Mya has to say."

He nodded and left.

I glanced at Kerr, who was still beside me. As usual, he was watching me. Although I was starting to read into some of his expressions, he seemed closed off now.

"Thank you for your company, Cassie. I will see you in the morning."

He left without any yearning look or inappropriate gesture. A pang of disappointment shot through me. Mya, who was watching me closely, gave me a small, knowing smile.

As soon as the door closed behind the fey, Hannah flopped onto the couch.

"What exactly was the plan for tonight? Get the fey drunk and see how desperate you could make them?" Mya asked, looking at Hannah.

"Come on, Mya. Everything was just fine," Emily said.

"Really? For you maybe. What about them? You bring them here, laugh and have fun, then say no to a simple request like saying goodnight?" Mya asked. "You're toying with them. You know what they want."

Hannah sighed loudly.

"Mya, I already gave it a try. I kissed Shax, and it wasn't anything special. What's the point of repeating it and unnecessarily getting his hopes up? Shax is just too nice. There was no spark."

"You're looking for someone who's more of an ass?" Mya asked.

Mya's determined pursuit of the topic would have made

me uncomfortable if Hannah hadn't dramatically rolled her eyes.

"There's no magic insta-love button that you can push, Mya. Falling for one of them is just like with human men. Personality and physical attraction. Yes, the fey are nice. But, physically, these guys have a lot of differences a girl needs to get over. They aren't as easy to fall in love with as you want them to be."

I took what was left of my cup of wine and sat down by Hannah. I was liking this girl more and more.

"You're right. If there's no spark, then that's fine. But, did you let Shax know that you're no longer interested?" Mya asked.

"Yes, I let him know. But, you know how well that goes over. Just look at Cassie. She told Kerr no, and he's still following her around."

Mya rubbed her head. I looked at her closely, noting the pale ring around her lips and the dark circles under her eyes.

"Headache?" I asked.

"Always," she said softly.

Eden started stacking the wine boxes by the door. Mya caught me watching her.

"This is exactly why we needed to talk to you," Mya said. "There's so much that the fey don't know. Like what alcohol can do to a person's personality. When you're out there, they're going to keep you physically safe, but you need to keep them mentally safe."

"What do you mean?" I asked.

"They're fascinated by things they don't understand or have a name for," Mya said.

"Like dildos," Eden piped in. "Do you know how many dildos and vibrators I had to clean out of Ghua's house? You can still smell the smoke of those suckers in the back."

I stared at the girl in disbelief.

"I'm counting on you to make sure we don't have another situation with sex toys, porn magazines, alcohol, or worse," Mya said.

"On top of trying to stay alive while looking for my son, husband, and supplies," I said dryly. I took a larger sip of my wine. What the hell had I signed up for?

"It won't be as hard as it sounds. When you're out there, you're going to turn into the group's mom," Mya said. "If they're doing something they're not sure you'd approve of, they'll be just like kids. If a fey looks guilty, ask him what he's hiding."

"Trust me. It works," Eden said. "And it's entertaining as hell when they're caught. Well, it's entertaining now. I might not have been so amused at the time."

"You want me to go around scolding almost seven-foot tall men, who more than double my weight and can rip off someone's head as fast as I can blink, like they're children?"

"Not scold. Just tell them to put back whatever they have," Mya said. "Or let Molev know."

"Molev?"

"Yeah, it's his turn to make a trip. Drav will be in charge here while he's gone. Molev's not expecting Merdon or

Thallirin back anytime soon, so there's no reason for him to stay."

She studied me for a moment.

"Molev makes you nervous?" she asked.

"They all do."

"Even after spending the day with Kerr? I thought it would help you be less nervous about tomorrow."

"You mean about leaving?"

"Yes. Leaving. Being with a fey. Trusting them to respect 'No' when you say it."

I considered it for a moment and nodded slowly.

"I guess I am less nervous about them. Although Molev is still the scariest, by far."

"No way," Hannah said. "Have you seen Merdon and Thallirin? Those guys are the scariest."

Having been focused on treating Merdon's leg wound, I hadn't really noticed more than their size and scars. It was Molev's stoic, larger-than-life presence and his position of authority that intimidated the hell out of me.

"There's really nothing to worry about with the fey. They'll keep you safe," Mya said.

I wondered if she felt like a broken record delivering the same message again and again.

"Well, I'm really more nervous about what I'll find out there," I finally admitted.

The mood in the room shifted. The smiles faded, and all the girls took a seat, watching me with sad eyes.

"It's possible, you know," Eden said after a moment. "To

survive out there. We're all proof of that. Don't give up hope."

"Hope? Hope left the moment I first saw the hellhounds." I drank the last of my wine and set the cup aside. "I just need to know what happened to Lee and Caden so I can put my thoughts to rest and focus on Lilly and surviving." I said the words, knowing that was exactly what I needed to do. However, I wondered if I'd be able to do it when I finally found what was left of them.

FROM MY SEAT at the kitchen table, I watched yet another fey pass the window. The number of men lingering outside Julie's house astounded me.

"Would you like some more cereal?" Julie asked.

I looked at Lilly, who was happily munching away on her current bowl, and knew Julie meant me.

"No, thank you. I'm good for now."

After returning from Hannah's house, I'd spent the night reading books to Lilly and teaching her ABCs like I had Kerr. The tales she'd told of her adventures with Timmy had brought a smile to my face, and I knew she'd be happy enough while I was gone. Still, I dreaded leaving.

I left the table to bring my bowl to the sink. The yard was now empty.

"Where did the fey go?"

"The hunting party is probably back," Julie said. "Would you like to go see what supplies they've brought?"

"Yes," Lilly said before I could respond.

She pushed her bowl to the side and scrambled from her chair.

"Hey, get back here. We don't waste food," I scolded.

She quickly wolfed down the rest of her cereal then washed her hands while I took the dishes to the sink.

In less than five minutes, the three of us left the house. My stomach churned with anxiety as we walked down the road. I knew the plan. The fey would unload the supplies from the truck, make sure there was enough gas to hit the next station, and then we would go. How had the days gone by so quickly?

When we reached the wall, the fey already had a bucket brigade line, passing supplies from over the wall into the smaller ranch house just inside the wall. They moved the totes filled with cans and boxes and a variety of other items into the house.

"Let's go inside and help Mya and Eden sort," Julie said.

Inside, the two women stood around a large table. The last fey in the line stacked totes on the floor around them. Other fey, inside the house, put the things that Mya and Eden handed them on different shelves.

I looked around in awe at all the supplies. Against one wall, I spotted a tower of stacked boxed wine.

"Is this the supply shed?"

"We needed to use a house so nothing would freeze," Julie said. "We thought saying 'supply shed' when talking to Matt would make it less hoarder sounding."

I snorted a laugh.

"I can see why you wouldn't want him to think you have a house full of supplies."

"It doesn't stay full," Mya said. "We sort through everything and give half to Whiteman. We also go through and add to their share more of whatever we're not using a lot of here."

"I'm not complaining or judging," I said. "I think it's more than fair when they're barely going out on their own supply runs anymore."

The way the people of Whiteman expected the fey to work 'round the clock to keep the survivors fed and safe was one of the main reasons Mya convinced Molev to move his people to Tolerance. Both sides had made publicly loud and valid points. Mya's argument that the fey were not slaves and had as much right to rest as the humans resonated with many of the survivors. Anyone with eyes could see how hard they worked. Matt's rebuttal that he was not asking the fey to do anything more than he was asking the overworked survivors to do had fallen on Mya's deaf ears. And, I couldn't fault her for that.

Matt might not be asking for more, but the fey had been and still were doing three times the work of the folks at Whiteman. Matt knew how valuable the fey were. Which is why Matt had pulled what he did with me. He knew the workload was unfair. Yet, what could he do about it? No matter how hard he pushed the survivors, they were still human and unable to do what the fey could do so quickly.

I got to work helping Mya and Eden sort supplies. While

we sorted, the empty totes were taken out and boxes were packed with supplies for Whiteman.

In no time, everything was done; and I stood back to watch Lilly, who was happily eating her way through a package of chocolate chip cookies with Mya's help.

"She'll be fine," Julie said softly. "No matter what. I'll make sure of it."

I nodded and swallowed hard, knowing I needed to leave quickly. A drawn-out farewell wouldn't help either of us.

Crossing the room, I planted a kiss on the top of Lilly's head.

"Be a good girl, Lilly-bean. I'll see if I can find some more cookies while I'm gone."

Forgetting her treats, she popped up on her chair and threw her arms around me.

"Stay quiet and run hard, Mommy, and they won't get you. I love you always."

Those were the words I'd told her every time the fence was breached back at Whiteman.

Trying not to cry, I kissed the top of her head again.

"I'll be back in a week. Have fun with Timmy, and try not to eat all of Mya's chocolate."

Lilly nodded and let me go.

I turned quickly and walked away before she could see my tears.

CHAPTER TEN

BLINDED BY MY TEARS, I SHUFFLED OUT THE DOOR. STRONG arms scooped me off my feet, and with a squeak, I blinked up at Kerr in surprise. He studied my face then slowly lowered his head. My heart jackhammered in my chest, and I held my breath. In that moment, I wanted his mouth on mine. It didn't matter if that yearning was from desire or simply the need to distract myself from the pain of leaving my daughter behind. I tipped my head toward his to let him know I was ready.

Kerr's arms tightened around me, and a faint rumble came from his throat.

However, instead of kissing me, he set his forehead to mine.

"Do not cry, Cassie. This is not a forever goodbye."

His hand moved against the jeans covering my leg.

"I swear on my life that you will see your daughter again."

I nodded, and uncomfortable with the intensity reflected in his gaze and my own need for comfort, ducked away from his touch.

He grunted and took off running toward the wall. My stomach flipped as he jumped over it. With a slight thump, he landed lightly beside a large, drab-green military-looking truck. Fey were passing empty totes into the back of it.

Kerr set me on my feet just as a human young man came around the back of the truck. He smiled at me and started jogging toward us.

"Hey, I'm Ryan," he said, coming to a stop before me.

"I'm Cassie. You must be Julie's son."

"I am. It's nice to meet you. Molev told me you're going out with the next group and will be driving. Let me show you around the truck, then we'll take it for a quick test spin."

"Sounds good. I don't think I've ever driven anything this big before."

The bottom of the driver's side door, which Ryan opened for me, was about neck level. There was a cupholder with a new bottle of water hanging from the door.

"It's not as bad as it looks. It's automatic, so there's really not much of a difference between driving this and a car. Well, other than the suspension and the ability to run things over. And, it rides rough going over some of the stuff the infected leave in the road. So, be sure to hang on tight."

His words caused the already large ball of anxiety in my stomach to grow larger. What would I find when we drove away from Tolerance. Back at Whiteman, I'd once glimpsed a horde of infected from a distance as they clawed at the fence.

That was the last time they'd managed to break in, and I never wanted to see that many infected again. The idea that I probably would in the next few days made my knees weak as I climbed into the cab and waited for Ryan to close the door.

Ryan nodded to Kerr, who remained in his spot. Kerr's gaze held mine as Ryan ran to the other side and got in. There was no fear in the fey's eyes, but our conversation about fearing what lay outside the walls rang in my head.

"Ready?" Ryan asked, closing the door.

In just a few minutes, I was familiar with all of the controls. Ryan stressed that I needed to use the windshield wiper as often as necessary to get rid of infected goo. There was spare fluid in the back. And he made sure I knew how to use the parking brake when the load was heavy, and I had to stop on an incline.

For the test drive, he only had me go down the road and back. It didn't take very long, but my stomach churned the whole time. It felt wrong to do anything outside the fence. However, I didn't see a single infected.

"Are there really no infected around here?"

Ryan grinned.

"The fey tend to keep them away. We haven't seen an infected in this area since two days after the fey moved in. No traps or tricks either. I think the infected are catching on to the fact that they can't win against the fey. At least, the ones in this area. Those still here tend to stay in the woods closer to Whiteman."

Hearing that made me feel marginally better about leaving Lilly in Tolerance with Julie and the other Fey.

I parked the truck in front of the wall and cut the engine.

"You'll do great," Ryan said. "Good luck, and drive safe."

He got out and left the door open.

Molev filled the opening and climbed up into the passenger seat.

"Are you ready, Cassie?" he asked.

"I'm as ready as I'm going to be."

He handed me a stack of maps and placed a lunch box on the seat beside me.

"We will clear the road ahead of you. Only stop if you need something."

With a tightness in my chest and sweaty palms, I started the truck as soon as he got out. The fey kept out of my way as I turned around then jogged alongside me once I started down the road that led away from Tolerance.

Turning onto Highway 13, I was surprised to see the road clear of vehicles. Then again, considering what the wall around Tolerance was made of, a clear road made sense. As we got further away, cars sat on the shoulder, vacant and doors closed, a fresh layer of snow helping to blend them with the landscape. Some of the windows were smashed, but nothing seemed out of the ordinary, considering the current state of the world.

The fey had no trouble keeping up with me. I felt bad for going the speed limit, but I really wanted to get to the first stop as soon as possible. According to the conversation with Mya and Eden the night before, the fey could run tirelessly for an entire day. Not that I wanted to test that.

With unobstructed roads, my thoughts wandered to what

we might find when we reached Parsons. Lee had considerately told me where he was taking Caden the night he had left. Having his new girlfriend's address hadn't reassured me at the time, but it did now. I knew where to look for my son.

Thirty minutes into the drive, I noticed something further down the road. The fey running lead noticed too and raced ahead, creating distance at a speed I wouldn't have thought possible. Instead of trying to keep up with them, I slowed down.

As they reached the pickup truck barricading both lanes, I lifted my foot from the gas completely. The snow, which had been pristine up until this point, was dotted with foot prints and drag marks around the truck even before the fey reached it.

My heart started to thunder as I realized what lay before us.

The doors of the truck swung open, and an infected stepped out. Even with the windows rolled up and the heat turned on low, I could hear the awful sound of its call. The low groaning-moan was cut short as one of the fey removed its head.

It didn't matter, though. The infected had done what it needed to do.

From the sides of the road, more infected poured from the trees. My heart started to hammer, and I stepped on the brakes. My door opened suddenly, and I screamed. With wide eyes, I stared at Kerr.

"Keep driving, Cassie," he said. "My brothers will move the vehicle before you reach it."

He closed the door before I could respond.

I stared at the infected swarming the road and all the fey fighting them. With effort, I pulled my gaze from the slaughter and glanced at Kerr still beside the door. He motioned me to start forward. As I removed my foot from the brake, my stomach churned, and I felt like I was going to throw up. But I did what he wanted and pressed down on the gas. The truck lurched forward, gaining speed.

Two fey stopped fighting long enough to push the vehicle off the road. The infected didn't notice me coming, but the fey did. I saw them look at me. None of the fey moved out of the way, though.

I glanced at Kerr, running beside me. He waved me forward.

"You can do this, Cassie." I tightened my grip on the steering wheel.

The fey waited until the last second to jump out of the way. The truck plowed through a swarm of infected. Blood splattered the windshield, and I fumbled with the wiper knob.

After that, I kept a relatively steady speed, only slowing slightly when spotting obstacles in the road. I let the fey move the stuff too big to drive over and plowed through the rest. The truck seemed to handle it very well. The driver not as much.

By the time we reached the first town we planned to check, my hands shook nonstop. It was barely mid-morning.

I pulled over to the shoulder, right in front of the sign that stated Clinton's population. The forerunners continued ahead, scouting the area. I cut the engine and looked at the houses to my right. The vacant homes gave me the creeps.

I leaned my head against the steering wheel and exhaled shakily. I didn't like stopping this close to town, but Mya and I had talked about it the night before. I needed to park at the edge of town and go in on foot because the noise of the truck would call too many infected to the area. I hated that parking further away would mean investing more time in each stop. Time I didn't want to sacrifice. I didn't want to sacrifice myself, either, though. Yet, that's what it felt like I was about to do, going in on foot.

Mya had promised it would be safe. However, after seeing all the infected on the way, I wasn't so sure anymore.

The sound of my door opening didn't make me jump this time.

"Are you all right, Cassie?"

I lifted my head to look at Kerr.

"My nerves are shot. I can't stop shaking. How do you guys do this?"

He looked at the fey around the truck.

"The same way you are doing this. Because you must."

I nodded and moved to get out. Instead of stepping back, Kerr reached up and lifted me down. He was too quick to set me on my feet this time. I would have rather stayed in his arms with a few comforting pets.

"You did not drink any water," he said. He reached around me and plucked the bottle from the cup holder.

"Drink."

"Then, I'll have to pee." I glanced at the open area on the side of the road. "I really don't want to have to pee."

He grunted and uncapped the water, handing it to me with an insistent nudge.

I gulped down two swallows and returned it to the cupholder.

"Take the bags from the back," Molev said, returning with the forerunners. "The way ahead looks clear."

His words sent a shiver through me, and I yearned for the secure walls of Tolerance.

"Come, Cassie," Kerr said. "I will carry you."

I gratefully let him scoop me up and held on tightly as he, along with a large portion of the group, took off down the road. The soft crunch of footsteps in the snow sounded loud in the silence surrounding us, and the group alertly watched for anything the noise might attract.

Before anything came our way, the highway split into double lanes. It should have been crowded with cars like the road had been on the way here. Instead, everything had already been moved off to the sides and was covered in snow. Was it because someone had already come through and picked the town clean? Or was it because infected had set up some sort of trap ahead? The virgin snow covering the pavement didn't give me an answer either way.

A sign to the left caught my attention.

"Kerr, we need to check that building," I said, pointing at the large brick structure. Finding a hospital this close to the edge of town was pure luck. I just hoped that wouldn't be the only bit of luck we had today.

The fey veered that direction, crossing over the lanes and running through the snow toward the hospital. The front windows of the first wing of the building were broken open, and the floor inside was dusted with snow.

"Wait here," Molev said. "We will check for infected first."

The majority of the group waited outside with Kerr holding me in their center. He didn't seem to mind that I had an arm looped around his shoulder or that I leaned into his warmth. My breath misted in the cold air, but I didn't complain. Outside in the cold was better than inside with any infected.

It wasn't long before Molev returned and waved us forward.

"We found a room with many pill bottles like Mya showed us."

He led the way to a large space that looked like it had once been a nice pharmacy attached to the hospital. Most of the shelves were empty, and the protective barrier behind the counter was smashed.

Given the state of things, I half expected to find empty shelves when Kerr took me around to the back. However, there was a lot of medicine left.

"Take anything that is not an empty bottle or container."

I wouldn't know what most of it was even if I read the label, but any medicine was better than no medicine. That one of the fey found a book under the counter with descriptions of most of the common pills was a bonus.

As soon as they had everything in bags, Molev motioned

the group toward the door. I expected us to return to the entrance. Instead, he continued the search for medical supplies. I knew it was logical to keep looking. We hadn't run into any trouble, and the pharmacy had supplied us with a good deal of medicine. But, Whiteman and Tolerance needed more than that. Sutures, bandages, and other supplies. However, I wondered if we were being smart. How much longer would our luck hold out?

Each corner we turned, my heart pounded a little harder. I kept expecting to see a barricade or an infected shambling towards us. But the halls were eerily empty.

Locked supply closets, drawers, or cabinets were not a problem for the fey. They broke into any space that might have something useful. And, often, it did.

Being inside the cold, dark building was fraying my nerves, though. There were just too many supplies left in the building for it to have been cleaned out by the fey or Whiteman's crews. That meant the cars on the road hadn't been moved by humans.

As soon as I found enough sutures to last Whiteman for a while, I called a halt to the search. Molev nodded and led the way out of the building. I clutched Kerr tightly, glad that he'd kept me in his arms the entire time, and I didn't take a normal breath until we stood outside.

Several fey ran the supply bags back to the truck while the rest of us continued in the direction we had started. It felt only marginally safer to be in the daylight with space to run. The lack of businesses on this side of town made it apparent, though, that there wasn't much more for us to scavenge unless we wanted to go into homes.

Molev stopped in the middle of the road and held up his hand. The group stopped and stood there in silence.

I pressed a little closer to Kerr. His hand against my leg made a soothing motion that didn't quite do the trick. My pulse was jackhammering too hard. My eyes darted around, searching the buildings, the shadows, and the snow for any sign of infected.

Without a word, the fey turned around and sprinted back toward the truck. I watched over Kerr's shoulder, but nothing appeared.

It wasn't until we reached the truck that I found my voice.

"What was wrong back there? Did Molev see something?"

"No, I didn't," Molev said from beside us, startling me. I'd been focused on Kerr and the fey loading the supplies into the back of the truck.

"The infected near Tolerance avoid us because they know they will die. However, infected everywhere else still try to attack us or trap us. We have yet to find a town as quiet as this one. Something is wrong here."

I couldn't have agreed more. My gut was telling me to run far and fast. Although, to be fair, it'd been telling me that since the moment Kerr jumped over Tolerance's wall with me this morning.

"Then, we'll skip any more scavenging here and continue on," I said.

"Yes. I think that is for the best."

Molev opened the door, and Kerr set me on the step-up. After a quick map check, I started the engine. The fey ran ahead, retracing our steps. Just after the hospital, I took a left and followed 13 along the outskirts of town.

At first, it seemed like we were heading away from town. But, it didn't take long for houses to pop up on both sides of the double-laned road. Too many houses not to attract some infected attention at the sound of the truck's passing. Yet, nothing came.

The further I drove, the more the cars jumbled the outer lanes instead of the shoulders, creating a channel. Someone did this on purpose. Why? My hands clenched the steering wheel, and I waited for something to move. For those car doors to open and let infected out like before.

When I came to an intersection with a fast food sign on the corner, I took a moment to wipe my sweaty palms on my jeans. Molev's words kept replaying in my head. None of this felt right. Where were the infected?

We passed another pharmacy on the left. There wasn't a single car in the parking lot, yet the snow on the ground was churned to a grey slop. Footprints and drag marks. The first signs of infected, more numerous than I'd ever seen, terrified me. I pressed down on the gas and sped past.

The front door of the pharmacy burst open, and infected came streaming out, the noise of their groans reaching me inside the cab. I watched in the mirrors as most of them shambled after the sound of the engine. Some of them actually ran, though. They scared me more than anything.

I forced the truck to go a little faster. Ahead, I saw a

familiar sign for one of the larger chain super centers. It would be another perfect place to grab supplies we desperately needed, but there was no way in hell I was stopping. A glance in the mirror showed that the infected from the pharmacy were still giving chase.

Movement ahead of the truck drew my attention, and I watched another swarm of infected pour from the super center as well. They ran in a group, coordinated and focused on the truck and my fey escort.

"Shit." I floored it.

The fey running ahead of the truck sprinted faster, outdistancing the vehicle to meet the infected. Like the trap on the road, the fey met the infected head-on and fought with bloody ferocity until I was almost on top of the struggling mass. At the last moment, the fey jumped out of the way. Infected, not smart enough to do the same, were crushed under the tires of the truck or splattered on the grill. Gore coated my windshield, and I deftly turned the wipers on.

Rumbling past, I watched the mirrors. The majority of the fey were swallowed by the crush of infected still joining the fight from behind and to the side. Shock had my foot easing up on the gas.

Something thumped on my door as a shape rose to eye level.

"Do not stop for anything, Cassie," Kerr ordered through the glass.

I floored it and barreled away from the fight. My eyes bounced between the view of the road ahead of me and the fight behind me. Heads and bodies flew. So many. After a moment, infected began to break away and run back toward the stores. At the infecteds' retreat, the fey split away and followed in the truck's wake.

How many times would this happen before I returned to Tolerance? How many times could this happen before I didn't return to Tolerance?

I drove steadily for fifteen minutes before Molev gave the signal to stop. With shaking hands, I pulled over to the shoulder and parked the truck. I opened the door without killing the engine, though. At the first sign of infected, I wanted to be ready to take off again.

"Was anyone hurt?" I asked Kerr. He looked at Molev, who came running up to the side of the truck.

"Nothing serious enough to address now," Molev said. "We should send a group back for supplies. That larger building is one that usually has much food."

I shook my head.

"Given the number of infected that came out of it, it wouldn't be worth the risk. There's a lot of towns we're going to pass through yet. We'll have other opportunities."

He grunted. Whether in agreement or not, I wasn't sure.

"Was that normal?" I asked. "How do the infected know to hide in stores now? Do they really understand that we're after the supplies in there, or was it just luck?"

"It is troubling," he said, looking back the way we'd come. "The infected seem to be getting even smarter."

"Yeah. Seems like it."

Molev walked away without confirming anything, and Kerr hopped up onto the step so he was towering over me.

"Drink some more water, and eat something from the bag next to you."

I looked at the lunch box. I knew I needed to eat but wasn't sure if I could. Half the fey and the front of the truck were still covered in infected bits. Hard to have an appetite around all of that glop. Instead, I grabbed the water and made a show of drinking.

Kerr nodded and hopped down. As soon as the door closed, Molev signaled for the forerunners to go. I capped the water and started up again, wondering what the next run-in would bring.

CHAPTER ELEVEN

Once Molev signaled that we were going to be stopping for the night, I thought I would be relieved. Instead, I now watched the encroaching dusk with trepidation as I followed the fey down a dirt road off the highway.

Today had been a new level of hell in survival. The infected lying in wait in Clinton hadn't been the last group we'd encountered like that. The undead were definitely getting smarter and had taken to lying in wait at places that had supplies. I didn't know how anyone would be able to scavenge on a large scale now. Whiteman would be screwed soon.

Molev motioned for me to park, interrupting my dismal thoughts. I let the truck idle while several small groups of fey checked each of the nearby country homes. Lights flickered on in all three. Molev waved me toward the grand, two-story with snow-covered planters standing sentinel at the end of the driveway.

I cut the engine at the garage and watched the fey jog around the yard to check the outbuildings and nearby trees. The garage door opened to show two shiny new cars. The fey inside called to Kerr that the house was safe.

Kerr looked up at me through the window and reached for the door. He'd run beside the truck the whole day. He had to be tired. Yet, he reached up for me and lifted me down as if it were nothing.

"Are you hungry?" he asked.

"Not really."

I'd given the same answer at lunch, not that it had done me any good. I'd still ended up eating inside some trashed house on the side of the road. Blood had smeared a few of the doors, and the water hadn't worked. But I'd been safe enough, thanks to the fey, and still able to use the bathroom. I just closed the lid instead of flushing. Something I'd gotten very good at since the first hellhound sighting all those weeks ago.

I felt sure this house wouldn't be much different, which made it hard to be hungry or to want to stop and rest. But, my nerves were shot, and I couldn't stop shaking. Far too many infected had tried chasing us down today.

"Come. We'll find something to eat from the supplies."

He picked me up and headed toward the back of the truck. It would have felt good to stretch my legs if they weren't acting like they were made of Jell-O. Being carried gave me a moment to try to stop the tremors running through me. Kerr seemed to notice because his fingers made soothing little circles on the side of my thigh until he reached the cargo doors.

With a boost, Kerr helped me into the cargo hold. Someone had been smart enough to install hooks every several feet along the top and bottom of the support bars. Cargo straps were fastened from hook to hook, holding all the stacked goods in place.

I looked at the supplies we had gathered so far, knowing most of what was there without actually seeing it. The truck was already a quarter full. We had even collected a fair amount of chocolate from a convenience store in Montrose, which filled at least two totes. A decent supply of spices and seeds from a market in Butler filled another four. Most of that was luxury instead of necessity. However, we'd also scored cases of jars and other canning supplies, along with an assortment of jellies. It wasn't the food and formula and diapers we needed, but the seeds for a garden and the canning supplies would help us next year, if we lived that long.

In the jumble of supplies, I spotted a few cans of chicken on top of a tote that someone must have found at the convenience store. I picked them up and showed them to Kerr.

"There really isn't much here to make a real meal," I said. "I'm sorry. I know two cans of chicken won't go very far."

He made no comment as he lifted me down and carried me straight into the house, the garage door closing behind us.

Inside, the fey were exploring the home. It felt safe

enough in there, and it was warm. I'd never been more grateful for a house with heat.

Kerr stepped into the kitchen where one of the fey was digging through the freezer. He started tossing packages to another man near the table. That fey set each frozen item on the surface with a solid thunk.

"Can we eat any of these?" Kerr asked.

"It looks like fish and beef. It should be okay as long as it doesn't smell bad when you thaw it."

He set me on my feet, and I moved to look for pans.

Kerr stopped me with a firm hand on my arm.

"Sit. Eat." Another fey threw a can opener to him.

While the fey moved around the kitchen, I sat at the table and ate the chicken from the cans that Kerr opened for me. I watched a fey dump all the frozen meat into a pot along with a few cups of water before lighting the stove. I couldn't imagine what that was going to taste like.

Each cupboard was opened and emptied of anything that resembled a food item. Those items the fey took straight outside to the truck.

All the while, the sky grew progressively darker. I only managed to finish a few bites before I pushed the first can aside.

A distant howl reached my ears, and I froze. My eyes locked on the window where the last light of the day was only a memory. There'd be no resting once the sun set. Not in this house.

"Do we have to stay here?" I asked.

Kerr held out his hand.

"There is a room upstairs where you can sleep."

Not arguing, I followed Kerr out of the kitchen and spotted fey settling down on the floors or any open piece of furniture, seemingly undisturbed by the sound of the hellhound. Maybe they knew it was too far away. I hoped that was the case. We reached a lit set of stairs leading up. It was the only surface without a fey sprawled on it. I looked at the top landing and didn't see any fey up there, either.

"Why isn't anyone upstairs?" I asked.

"Mya told us that you might like privacy at night."

I swung my gaze to his.

"Nope. Not even a little. I'll sleep down here."

Kerr nudged me up the stairs, anyway.

"I heard it," I said. "The hellhound."

"You're safe. Nothing will harm you. I swear."

I didn't believe him. Not for a moment.

"It doesn't feel safe sleeping by myself," I said.

"I promise you are safe."

When I stubbornly crossed my arms, he picked me up and carried me the rest of the way upstairs.

I waited until we reached the landing to struggle out of his hold. I wasn't stupid enough to risk us both falling to our deaths on the stairs.

"You can't just take my choices from me."

He released me easily but frowned when I crossed my arms and didn't continue down the hall.

"You're tired," he said. "Your skin is so pale the marks on your nose seem darker. The skin under your eyes looks grey like Tor's." He gently reached up and traced under my left eye.

"I will not leave you alone," he said softly. "I will stay with you all night if it will help you feel safe."

He held out his hand, and I knew he was asking for me to do more than accept his offer. He wanted my trust, too. I placed my hand in his and let him lead me to the bedroom at the end of the hall. The whole time, his thumb brushed the back of my hand.

I didn't mind the contact a bit.

A day of riding adrenaline waves from the constant threat of infected left me feeling two blinks away from collapse and terrified at the same time. After just hearing that howl, the last thing I wanted to do was give in to my need for sleep. Yet, when I saw the large bed, neatly made and very inviting, I couldn't help but shuffle toward the oasis.

I wouldn't sleep. Not with those howls distantly disturbing the night and every single light in the room on. But, I could lie down and let my body take a break.

I sank into the soft mattress and stared up at the ceiling. When was the last time I had a bed to myself? That thought gave birth to another. What was Lilly doing? Was she playing with the toys? Was she as terrified as I was? Missing me as much as I missed her?

Kerr sat on the floor near the door. When he'd said he would stay, I'd thought it would be next to me. My face heated a little at the thought of sharing the bed with him.

Exhaling slowly, I noted how completely at ease he appeared.

"Doesn't it bother you? Hearing the howls and knowing they're somewhere out there?"

"I don't remember a lifetime where I didn't hear them. This is nothing new."

I couldn't say hearing that made me feel any better. I didn't want to grow used to hearing the hounds. I wanted the old, safer world back, but as much as I wanted that, I knew it wasn't a possibility. There was no going back; only going forward. That was something I'd started telling myself after the old commander of Whiteman announced the bombing of all major cities.

"Close your eyes and rest," Kerr repeated.

"I can't. When I close my eyes, I see theirs. The glowing red in the darkness."

I remembered the first time the hounds attacked Whiteman. No one knew what was going on. The dark, sleek shadows with glowing red eyes came in and bit people. In the glimpse I'd caught, the hounds appeared very similar to greyhound dogs. Only taller, blacker, and with bits and pieces missing.

"Try, Cassie. You will not be able to drive tomorrow if you do not sleep."

He was right. Trembling, I closed my eyes. Instead of seeing hellhounds, I saw Lilly, alone in her bed.

THE BED MOVED. For half a second, I thought I'd crowded Lee out again. Not that I cared. He'd made it clear we weren't together; yet he still insisted on sharing a bed for Lilly's sake.

All the bitterness I felt vanished as I realized Lee wasn't with me. He was gone. So was Caden. And, I was looking for them.

I opened my eyes and looked around the dim room. Kerr stood by a window near the bed. As I watched, he pulled back the curtain an inch to peer outside. Sunlight streamed in.

I couldn't remember falling asleep. But I did remember I'd been in bed by myself. Was my mind trying to take me back to a time I felt safer, even if I'd been bitter about it? I reached my hand out under the blankets and paused. The spot beside me felt warm. Not only that, but I was fully under the covers and no longer wore my shoes. I wouldn't have taken off my shoes with the hound howling outside.

The light in the room dimmed again, and I looked up to meet Kerr's gaze.

"Did you take my shoes off?" I asked.

"You weren't sleeping well. I took your shoes off and helped you under the covers. You slept much better after that."

His consideration warmed me. I did feel rested. Really rested.

"How late is it?"

He shrugged, and I looked around the room and saw a watch on the opposite night stand. I slid across the bed, feeling his warm spot again, and checked the time.

"It's past nine," I said, throwing back the covers. "We need to go."

It wasn't like there was a ton of daylight to start with. Using some of it for something like sleep was unforgivable.

I used the attached bathroom to rush through a morning routine and joined Kerr in the kitchen less than five minutes later. He was at the stove with his back to me.

"Where is everyone?" I asked, looking around the empty house.

"A group returned to Butler to gather more supplies. They're at the other houses washing."

He set a cover on the counter, and I sniffed at the delicious smell suddenly teasing my nose.

"Sit," Kerr said.

He turned holding a pan of scrambled eggs.

"For real? They found eggs?"

I hurried to sit and eagerly watched him plate a large portion of the eggs.

"They smell amazing." I couldn't rip my eyes from their golden goodness. How long had it been since I'd eaten eggs like this? Ages. Eggs weren't my favorite food. At least, they weren't before the quakes. Now, they looked like stomach gold.

Just as I picked up my fork to take the first bite, Molev walked into the kitchen.

"Good morning, Cassie. Did you sleep well?"

"After a while I did," I answered absently. Unable to help myself, I forked a large bite and quickly shoved it into my mouth. Kerr had even salted them. I was in heaven.

Molev sat at the table and placed several maps in front of me.

"Can you show me the route you wanted to take today?"

I finished chewing and studied the maps.

We weren't far from Rich Hill. From there, we'd go down 49 to Nevada then over to hit Fort Scott. After Fort Scott, I planned to head to Parsons, avoiding all towns. I wanted to get as close as possible today so we could start out looking for Caden at first light tomorrow. It didn't look like a long distance on paper, but between stopping to hunt for supplies and infected traps, I knew it would take time.

Between bites of egg, I traced my finger along the route and pointed out the towns I thought we should search. Molev listened to my explanation and nodded when I finished.

"We will stop outside of Parsons tonight," he said.

My heart felt close to bursting. I couldn't wait to hold Caden again. The thought that I might not find him tried to nudge its way forward in my mind, but I pushed it back.

After I finished eating, I quickly washed my hands and took a big drink of water. Oddly, I felt less nervous today than I had the day before. Maybe it had something to do with finally sleeping more than a few hours at a shot. Maybe it was because I knew what to expect. Or, maybe it was because I was so close to finally having my answers. Whatever the reason, I strode out the door with confidence and climbed into the truck.

The engine roared to life, a call for the fey to gather. They were all clean once more. A few of them still had wet hair from recent showers.

It was a short, uneventful ride to Rich Hill. Although we were getting closer to the area that I knew well, Rich Hill wasn't part of it, yet. So, I was a little surprised I didn't notice the supermarket right off the highway until Molev signaled to stop. I immediately pulled over to the shoulder. Kerr was right there when I open the door.

Safely within his arms, I watched a small group of fey approach the store. There were a few moments of quiet, followed by a moan, then nothing.

A fey stepped outside and waved us in. I tried to ignore the two bodies near the entrance and the fresh black glop of the blood stains running down the walls. It was better than having a horde of them waiting for us.

Looking around at the shelves and items scattered on the floor, the store appeared well picked over. Obviously, a store this close to the highway made it an easier raiding target.

"How much room is left in the back of the truck?" I asked.

"More than half," Kerr answered. "Plenty of room for whatever we want to take from here."

I hadn't asked because we'd hit the mother lode. The shelves were mostly vacant, like the other stores we'd managed to check. The half-filled truck meant we weren't hitting the right stores. Was that why the infected had lain in wait at those other stores but not this one? Because of the abundance of supplies?

Shaking my head and focusing on the moment, I pointed to the aisle sign that said baby.

"Buh-ay-buh-why?" Kerr said.

"Very close," I said. "It's buh-ay-buh-ee. Sometimes the y can sound like an e."

He carried me to the baby aisle, and I found the infant toiletries untouched. The formula, however, was gone.

"Take all of this," I said with a wave.

Fey moved around us and started stripping the shelves bare.

"What is it?" Kerr asked.

"Mostly diapers. Babies use them instead of underwear until they learn to use the bathroom. If we can get into one of those bigger stores, hopefully we can find some cloth ones with pins."

"Why?"

"Babies go through a lot of diapers, and what's left in the stores won't last forever."

And it wasn't just Caden who would need the diapers. Angel's baby needed supplies, too. And, likely, hers wouldn't be the last baby born. I'd seen a few guards coming out of some of the single women's tents. I chewed my lip and looked around for condoms. I found them right next to the pregnancy tests. Surprisingly, both were untouched.

"We should take those too," I said, hoping Kerr wouldn't try to sound out the words on the packaging.

While the fey loaded the meager supplies in the back of the truck, I waited in the cab and drank some water under Kerr's very watchful eye. I considered him for a moment then decided to ask.

"Did you sleep next to me last night?"

Several of the fey, still moving supplies out of the store,

glanced our way. The tips of Kerr's pointed ears darkened, and he glanced at the ground.

"Yes. I wanted you to feel safe."

Had he acted possessive or given me some kind of long look that hinted at his continued interest in having a relationship, I would have suggested he stay on the floor the next time. But his blush and the way he tugged on his earlobe softened my answer to a simple, "Thank you."

He nodded and closed the door. It was hard to stop watching him after that awkward exchange.

CHAPTER TWELVE

As soon as everything was stowed, Molev signaled for me to start the engine again. We continued our way south toward Nevada.

My mind drifted between finding Caden and noticing the way Kerr's clothes hugged his muscular frame as he kept pace with the truck.

I tore my gaze from Kerr's impressive thighs when the forerunners' sudden increase of speed alerted me to trouble. I squinted at the dark shape in the road ahead, but I knew better than to slow down. Keeping my speed steady, I focused on the distant obstruction. A pile of cars from the looks of things.

The fey worked as a group to move the vehicles from the road. To my surprise, the first one they moved didn't slide over to rest on the shoulder but fell out of view. A bridge? No sooner had that car disappeared than infected poured out of the nearby trees and onto the road.

Like the day before, this group clustered around the fey in a coordinated effort. However, they still didn't stand a chance. The fey tore through the infected like they were swatting down flies. From within the jumbled mass of struggling bodies, heads flew in all directions.

I gripped the steering wheel tightly and braced myself as I plowed through those too stupid to move. The jolting ride over the bodies and the splatter on the windshield churned the eggs in my stomach. As soon as I was on the other side, I used the wipers to clear my view then took a drink of water to keep my breakfast down.

After that, the roads were relatively free of problems.

Closer to Nevada, I watched the signs I passed for any indication of a store worth raiding. I'd visited Nevada after Lilly was born and remembered bits and pieces of the town. I knew of a supercenter on the east side, not far off the highway. However, before I reached the fork to veer off near Joplin, I spotted a sign for a dollar store.

Excited, I took my foot off the gas and signaled so that the fey running behind me would know that I was pulling over. Someone called to Molev, and the forerunners turned around as I parked.

"What is it?" Kerr asked when I opened the door. "Are you hungry? Do you need to use a bathroom?"

I smiled at his concern.

"No. I'm okay. That's a type of supply store, too," I said, indicating the building beside us.

He grunted and lifted me down from the cab.

Like the supermarket, the dollar store had been picked

over as well. The useful things like razors and toothbrushes were missing along with anything edible. However, I found plenty of other supplies that Whiteman could use and some more baby essentials, including diaper pins and cloth diapers.

After making sure the back was infected-free, Kerr waited for me to use the bathroom and then returned me to the truck. I took a few minutes to grab a quick bite from the snacks Molev had left for me then started down the road once more.

Today was definitely shaping up better than the day before. It gave me hope for the next day. Maybe my luck was finally changing.

I took the fork to Joplin as I'd planned and skirted the rural, industrial side of Nevada. I hoped less houses and off the beaten path meant the infected hadn't swarmed the store, looking to set a trap.

Turning onto a road that paralleled the back side of the store, I cut the engine.

I smiled down at Kerr when he opened the door and readily hopped down into his embrace.

"I have a good feeling about this one," I said.

UNLIKE THE NIGHT BEFORE, I was more than ready to get inside the house Molev had found for me. The lights were on, and the guys were cleaning it out. I waited impatiently in Kerr's arms, trying to keep as still as possible. My skin itched. Probably from the dozens of baby wipes he'd scrubbed over every inch of my exposed skin when I'd accidently gotten splattered with infected blood.

I glanced at the truck, and the fey who was hosing it off, and shuddered.

"I'm sorry, Cassie," Kerr said, yet again.

"There's nothing to be sorry for. You guys were amazing. I just wasn't fast enough with the window. They came out of nowhere."

I patted Kerr's back with the arm wrapped around his shoulder.

"If not for you, I wouldn't be here. You're keeping your word Kerr. And I can't begin to tell you how grateful I am."

As soon as one of the fey waved that it was clear, Kerr carried me inside and set me on my feet.

"Point me to the nearest bathroom," I said to one of the fey who'd checked the house.

He indicated a door to our right. However, it was only a half bath.

"Is there one with a shower? I need to wash."

"Upstairs, Cassie. Third door on the left."

"Thanks."

Kerr moved to pick me up, but I stopped him.

"Can I walk this time? You can go first, though."

As soon as I said it, I thought of his butt and blushed. My staring had gotten me into a lot of trouble today.

Kerr was getting under my skin in a way he would probably celebrate. With all this carrying me around, gentle touches, and heart-melting consideration, of course I couldn't stop thinking about him. Or looking at him, apparently. I'd been mid-fantasy where Kerr had his shirt off and I'd been witness to every chiseled contour of his perfect abs when I'd grown just a little too warm. The vibrations in the truck seat hadn't helped cool my fantasy, either.

Rolling down the window shouldn't have been a big deal. I'd just timed it horribly wrong, and everything had happened so fast. Infected pouring from the trees, running right in front of me. The squishy noises. Kerr jumping up and shielding me after the first gush. Me, hanging onto the wheel for dear life while trying not to think of what had landed on my left sleeve.

I exhaled slowly, trying not to think of any of it, and kept my gaze focused on my feet when Kerr started up the stairs. It was a struggle not to look up at his ass. He had a very nice one.

Why was I having these thoughts? Why now? And why of Kerr? He was the last person I would have ever thought I'd be staring at the way I'd done most of today. I blamed it on him sleeping beside me the night before just so I would feel safe. Lee had never shown that level of consideration for my thoughts and feelings. Obviously not since he did ask me for a divorce when I was just a few weeks pregnant.

I needed to get my head on straight. I needed to focus on the task at hand. We were so close. Just outside of Parsons. First thing in the morning, we would start the search for my son. Maybe that's why I was distracting myself today? Because, even though I refused to think something might have happened to him, it was still there in the back of my mind.

That depressing thought had my footsteps slowing as I followed Kerr down the hallway, right past the third door. I said nothing as he walked into the master and checked the bathroom there before motioning me inside.

The soft click of the bathroom door closing brought me out of my dark thoughts. I looked around the modest room, noting how untouched everything was. Not wanting to dwell on what might have happened to the people who once lived here, I turned on the water and waited a minute to see if it would warm. To my surprise, it did.

I eagerly stripped out of my dirty clothes and stepped into the steaming spray of water. It felt like heaven. And, I realized that since living with the fey, a lot of things had started feeling like heaven. Sleeping in a house and in a real bed. Feeling safe. Eating foods I never thought I'd eat again. And showering. Things that I'd taken for granted in my life before the earthquakes...but never again. I'd treasure each normal moment and commit it to memory for when moments weren't so normal.

I used the body wash on the shower shelf and soaped up twice. After I rinsed, I conditioned my hair for the first time in ages. Another heavenly moment.

When I turned off the water, the darker thoughts that wanted to weigh on my mind were further from the surface, despite the dimming light outside the bathroom window. I found a towel and dried off, enjoying the feeling of being clean and warm.

It wasn't until I had wrapped my hair that I realized my

mistake. All I had were the dirty clothes piled on the floor, and I really didn't want to put any of those back on.

I glanced at the door and tugged the towel from my hair. This wouldn't be the first time I had to make a naked, mad dash for clothing. Although, previous instances had been post-sex and not wanting to get caught by Lilly. Definitely a lifetime ago.

With the towel securely wrapped around me, I cracked the door open an inch. The bedroom door was now closed and the room empty. I remembered Kerr's comment about privacy the night before and thanked my good luck.

With the coast clear, I hurried to the dresser. I found clean underwear, some sweatpants, and a t-shirt. It didn't matter that they were all men's clothing. Clean underwear was clean underwear. I dropped my towel, intent on dressing before Kerr knocked for dinner.

A low moan came from behind me as I bent to step into the underwear. I spun around in terror, one hand at my throat and the other in front of me as if I could stave off an infected attack.

Instead of an infected, I saw Kerr standing just outside the walk-in closet. His hands were fisted at his sides and a set of women's clothes lay at his feet. Relief flooded me.

"Oh, thank God it's you." I placed my hand on my chest to subdue my heart's attempt at escape.

A slow darkness consumed his ears and spread to his face. He was cute when he blushed.

The reason why he blushed registered a moment later.

I gasped and slapped my hands over my breasts.

"I'm so sorry!"

His gaze dipped to the V of my legs. I hurried to move a hand down there and used my forearm for the girls. Kerr's gaze drifted up to my stomach. Lee had always hated my stretchmarks and wanted the lights off during sex. So, shame had me giving up the girls' coverage to shield my stomach. I didn't want Kerr to see the marks and think less of me. Halfway to my goal, I realized I didn't have enough arms to cover everything.

I half-turned my back to him while I struggled to figure out what parts were most important to cover.

In a few large steps, Kerr crossed the room and grabbed my hands, stopping my dilemma. His thumbs stroked the backs of my hands as he held my gaze.

"Never be sorry. Seeing you just now was like seeing the surface for the first time. The wonder of it stole every thought and will never leave me."

He pressed his forehead to mine and inhaled deeply.

"I know you can have no other man in your life now."

He released one of my hands to cup my head, his fingers stroking my scalp.

"I am patient and will ignore this burning need I have for you until you are free. Then, you will be mine."

He pulled back enough to press his lips to my forehead then turned and quietly left the room. I stared at the closed door in wide-eyed shock. Tingling need swept through me.

Then, you will be mine.

The phrase played on repeat in my head.

I should have been horrified that he'd seen me naked or

that he hadn't taken my no as a permanent no. Instead, a little part of me jumped up and down that he'd seen everything and still had a "burning need" for me. The shock left my face, and I grinned stupidly at the door.

I crossed the room and picked up the clothes he'd dropped. The underwear were a pretty pink. They wouldn't have fit me weeks ago but snugly covered me now. And, the sports bra matched perfectly. I slipped the soft sweater over my head then tugged on the jeans before pulling them off and switching to the sweatpants. The material would be more comfortable for sleeping.

As soon as I finished dressing, I went downstairs.

Kerr was in the kitchen, heating something on the stove. The other fey were milling around the house.

My eyes devoured the wide expanse of Kerr's snugly covered shoulders before dipping to his butt. I just couldn't help myself. Or the grin that wanted to curve my lips.

One of the fey passing through the room paused to look at me. Busted, I averted my gaze and approached Kerr.

"What's for dinner?" I asked, hating that I felt awkward now.

"Cheesy noodles. Do you like them?"

Kerr looked up from his stirring, his gaze sliding down my length then up again before meeting my eyes. His ears darkened again, and I felt myself blush, knowing where his thoughts had just gone.

"Honestly, I like most anything. Was there any meat in the freezer here?"

He shook his head.

"Can I help with anything?"

"No. Sit at the table and rest."

He ran all day and was telling me to rest? I smiled as he turned back to the stove.

The sound of the TV drew my attention, and I saw one of the fey had started a movie. The title for a violent action movie flicked on the screen.

I quickly went into the living room to find something else. The fey who'd started the movie watched me closely. I recognized him from Emily and Hannah's party. Tor. His skin was a bit lighter than most fey.

"I think Mya would prefer that you watch this one," I said to him. "The one playing is very violent."

I realized how ridiculous that sounded after the fey had spent the day ripping off people's heads, but I'd promised Mya that I would keep things PG.

Tor's gaze flicked to the case of the movie he'd picked then to mine.

"This one looks more interesting," he said, holding up the case that showed a well-endowed actress almost spilling out of her top while holding a gun.

"I know it does. But Mya made me promise to keep things PG."

"I like when Ryan is in charge."

I chuckled. His response and the way he sulkily changed the movies reminded me of Lilly.

"I'll be sure to mention that to Mya."

His sullen expression quickly changed to one of panic.

"Please don't."

"Tor," Kerr said.

I glanced his way in time to see him slowly shake his head.

Tor apologized to me.

"You didn't do anything wrong," I said. "Mya just wants to protect the way you guys are now."

"What do you mean?"

"You're all kind and loyal and protective. Traits that had been a little lacking in humans. Maybe she thinks the things we humans chose to expose ourselves to contributed to the slow decay of those traits."

"I understand."

Once he started the new movie, I went back to the kitchen where Kerr had two plates waiting on the table.

He and I ate together in silence, both casting not too subtle glances at each other. As soon as I took my last bite, he took our plates to the sink then held out his hand. This time, my stomach went hot and cold when I slid my fingers into his.

Neither of us spoke as he led the way upstairs. My trembling started anew as soon as we entered the bedroom, and he pulled back the covers. Holding them, he waited while I slid into bed. I had to look away from his intense gaze.

Instead of lying beside me like I know he had done the night before, he went to the door and sat in front of it. I rolled on my side so I could see him better.

"You're not going to lie next to me tonight?" I asked.

"I think you feel safe like this."

I couldn't deny it because I did. Yet, I also wanted him to lie beside me again.

"What do you think we're going to find tomorrow?" I asked softly.

He studied me before answering.

"We will find your husband and your son."

I was quiet for a moment then said what had been eating away at me for a long time.

"What if they're both dead? What if they're both infected?"

"In many ways, the humans and the fey are different; but in many more, we are the same. We grieve the loss of our brothers when they fall. If your husband and son have fallen, I will grieve their loss with you."

I swallowed past the lump in my throat and blinked at the moisture in my eyes. A tear slowly rolled down my cheek, and I nodded in silent thanks before closing my eyes.

I'd just begun to drift off when a baying clamor startled me awake. It wasn't just one hellhound out there but several. And they sounded far too close.

A door downstairs slammed.

I bolted upright and stared at Kerr. He stood and crossed the room. Slowly, he eased down on the bed beside me and opened his arms. I didn't hesitate to take what he offered. With his arms secure around me, I listened to the steady, calm beat of his heart.

"Nothing can get you while you're here."

I wasn't sure if he meant the house, at his side, or in his arms. Still shaking with fear, I closed my eyes and decided to believe all of the above.

Outside, men started shouting as the growls grew louder.

Footsteps thudded on the stairs. I found Kerr's hand and gripped it.

"Your hair smells sweet like the flowers from my home."

"W-what?"

I turned my head, not believing he was smelling my hair while at least two of those creatures were just outside.

He leaned in and rubbed his nose against mine.

"I know the hounds are outside, but I can't focus on them. Not when I'm here with you. Feeling your body against mine."

Maybe he had the right idea. Not thinking.

I turned further and pressed my lips to his. He groaned and held still until I opened my mouth and licked his bottom lip. He growled in the back of his throat, and his hold on me tightened.

I pulled back and looked at him. The vertical slits of his pupils were so wide they were almost round.

"I have no right to you," he said. "But I will fight until my dying breath to make you mine."

"Why?"

Glass shattered downstairs. Panicked, I kept talking to distract myself.

"I'm a mom with two kids. I'm emotionally bruised and not even sure if I want another relationship. I'm not sure I can trust someone with my heart like that again. On top of all my baggage, there's the fact that we barely know each other. Sure there's a physical attraction. A lot of it." I let my fingers wander over his hard chest for a moment. "And yes, I know I said motivations are more important than knowing each other, but that's not enough to build a future on."

Yelling and howls grew deafening.

"If it's even possible to have a future."

I couldn't stop shaking and burrowed my face against Kerr's chest. His hand smoothed over the back of my head again and again as my heart thudded in my ears. Tears flowed freely. I wanted to see Lilly again. I was so stupid for leaving her on the non-existent chance that Caden was still alive. This whole trip wasn't about finding him. It was about closure so my heart could stop feeling like it was being ripped out every time I thought of a tiny infected baby wriggling and hungry, forgotten on the floor of Lee's new girlfriend's house.

Lost in my desperate thoughts to see my daughter again, I didn't at first notice Kerr's murmured promises of safety or the silence outside. When I did, I swallowed my tears and listened. No hounds. No yelling.

I lifted my head to meet Kerr's gaze.

He groaned and pressed his mouth to mine. I didn't know if it was relief that I was alive, gratitude that he'd held me, over a year without sex, or the need for him that he'd slowly kindled inside of me. But, whatever it was, the touch of his lips set a fire in me. I grabbed him by the hair and kissed him back hard. The moment my tongue touched his, the bed started to shake.

Someone knocked on the door, startling me into breaking the kiss.

Kerr growled, and I found myself on my back with his hard length blanketing me. He set his forehead to mine. I barely felt it or the warm exhale that washed over my face. All I could feel was the press of his erection against my legs.

"Kerr, are you looking at her pussy?" a muffled voice called through the door. "Mya said we're not supposed to ask Cassie to see hers."

A heat like nothing I'd felt before flooded my face. Slowly, I looked up at the man pinning me to the bed.

CHAPTER THIRTEEN

"I saw her pussy yesterday," Kerr said. My mouth dropped open in shock, and his gaze dipped along with his head.

"It was as beautiful as Ghua promised. And covered with hair."

Before his lips could touch mine, I clapped my hand over his mouth and shook my head.

"It is beautiful," Kerr mumbled. "I would like to see it again. Many times."

"The hounds are gone," the voice called. "Cassie is needed. Molev and several others were injured."

Kerr rolled off of me and held out his hand. Instead of getting out of bed, I pulled the blanket over my face.

"Why are you hiding? The hounds are gone," Kerr said.

"I can't believe you described my downstairs to another guy. He's going to be picturing it every time he looks at me now."

"He is not going to try to picture your pussy because of my words. He was trying to picture it long before now."

I flipped back the cover to stare at him incredulously.

"Why would you say that?"

"Because it is true. Come. My brothers need you."

After the conversation we just had, I wasn't sure I wanted to leave the room. But, I still sat up and got out of bed, without Kerr's offer of help.

And when I left the room, I kept my eyes on the floor, not wanting to see the face of the fey waiting in the hall or anyone else who might have heard their exchange.

In the kitchen, several fey, including Molev, were sitting at the table. They looked like hell. Cuts and gashes showed through their ripped clothing and marred their exposed skin. Molev bled freely from his hand, the drip, drip, drip on the tile slowing even as I watched.

"I'll need the red totes out of the back of the truck. Those are the ones with all the medical supplies in them." A few fey moved to get what I needed.

I walked around the table, visually checking the injuries to determine which were the worst.

"Most of these wounds look like something I can stitch easily. I know soaping up won't feel good, but can you all take showers first? Use plenty of soap and wash twice to remove any hellhound saliva. When you're finished, grab any open bed, and I'll come to each one of you as soon as I can."

"Go," Molev said to the other two at the table. "I will wait until you're finished."

The pair nodded and left the room. I could see from the way they moved just how much they were hurting.

"Was it just you three injured?" I asked.

"No. Others were hurt but not badly enough to use the supplies meant for the people at Whiteman."

Molev's generosity and Matt's asshat attitude collided in my head.

"I think I'll be the judge of that," I said. I walked through the house and checked everyone. He was right about not needing to use the medical supplies. Most of the injuries were minor scratches that I knew would heal quickly on the fey. I still gave each man my time and advice on how to care for their wounds. However, I doubted the house would have enough soap for all the washing that would need to happen tonight.

When I returned to the kitchen, Molev was gone, and the totes were on the table. I dug for what I needed, handing a few items to Kerr, then went upstairs to start stitching the first fey, Bauts.

Kerr hovered closely, watching everything I did. And, like when I treated Merdon, Kerr handed me what I needed and removed any trash that might have infected blood on it. It was a long while before I straightened away and told Bauts he should stay in the bed and rest for the remainder of the night.

The second fey, Azio, lay bare-assed on a frilly white comforter in the next room. I took a child's blanket to modestly cover his hips then started stitching the worst of his wounds as well. Those I didn't stitch, I still probed for teeth.

By the time I reached Molev, my lower back was aching.

However, seeing the deep scores across his back now that he was laying on his stomach made my pain seem insignificant.

"What happened out there?" I asked to distract him.

"Two hellhounds found us. We pinned them and crushed their hearts. They will not be back."

"Why do they always hunt in pairs?" I gently started probing the worst of his wounds.

"I think it is because this place is so much larger than our caverns, and they want to cover more ground. Something they cannot do if they would continue to hunt in the large packs they are used to."

I opened the first suture package and set to work.

"They hunted in larger packs in the caverns?"

"Yes. I never encountered a pack of less than ten."

"I couldn't imagine how you would have been able to fight ten at a time."

"Most could not and died often."

I remembered Kerr's comment about lifetimes and stopped talking after that. Molev didn't move or make a sound as I worked. I knew it had to hurt, though. When I snipped the end of the final stitch, I noticed his eyes were closed and his breathing even. Thinking he was sleeping, I took a blanket from the end of the bed and covered him up. Kerr didn't say anything.

Molev, who I'd thought sleeping, said my name and startled a scream from me.

"I am sorry," he said. "I did not mean to frighten you."

He started to sit up, and I hurried to put a hand on his shoulder.

"You need to rest. Bodies, at least humans, heal faster that way."

"I will. But not here. This is your bed."

He tried to get up again, and I pushed him back down. I was no fool. I knew he had the strength to swat me aside, but the fey reserved that strength for the infected and the hellhounds.

"Molev, if you don't stay in this bed and sleep the rest of the night, I'm going to…"

He watched me expectantly.

"Okay, fine. I have no threat that will work with you. But I really want you to stay and get a good night's sleep. Tomorrow's the day we look for Caden. And with the way the infected are acting, everyone needs to be at their best. We'll be heading straight into the thick of it. No skirting around the edges tomorrow."

He grunted and closed his eyes. As I stared at him to make sure he was actually going to sleep, I realized I wasn't afraid of him anymore. He was the biggest and baddest of them all and standoffish compared to the rest, but he still had the same gentle qualities that made the fey who they were.

I moved away from the bed and found Kerr had placed a blanket on the floor. Was it just a lucky guess that he knew I wouldn't dream of kicking an injured man out of bed?

I crossed the room and lay down. He took a pillow from the bed and joined me. As exhausted as I was, the heat of his arm against mine sent me to sleep.

THE LIGHT PENETRATED my sleep after I turned my head. By slow degrees, I became aware of reality. Warm. Cuddled. Laying on top of a chiseled torso that definitely liked mornings.

My cheeks heated, and I lifted my head to look down at Kerr. His arms tightened around my waist. One hand moved between my shoulder blades. The other hand anchored my lower back and pressed my hips more firmly against his massive erection.

Not thinking clearly, I sat up quickly, straddling him. His hands locked on my hips. There wasn't enough material between us to shield my sensitive bits when he arched into my pelvis. A zing of pleasure hit me hard. A small sound escaped me. He pressed upward again, his gaze locked on my face. I barely managed to stop my eyes from rolling back in my head.

"You need to let go," I said, my voice quavering just a bit as I unintentionally rocked against him.

"For now." The low rumble of his words sent little aftershocks through me.

I stood and bolted toward the bathroom, turning scarlet when I noticed Molev sitting up in bed, watching me.

Within the safety of the bathroom, I rinsed my face and tried not to think about what I'd felt waking up in Kerr's arms like that, what Molev had witnessed, or what the day ahead might bring. However, that didn't leave me much to think about. So of course, I dwelled on all three until Kerr knocked on the door and told me it was time to go.

When I opened the door, I was alone in the room. The jeans from the night before waited on the dresser. Instead of changing into them, I kept the sweats on. Maybe they would remind me of my mom status and my need to chill my libido.

None of the fey looked at me differently when I walked downstairs, but I sure as hell felt different around them. Last night's pussy exchange had proven that they were worse than women when it came to sharing what went on in private. And, I was sure most of them already knew I'd just test rode Kerr like a pony.

I tried to keep my focus on the day ahead and took a helping of oatmeal from the small pot on the stove. Molev sat across from me. My mortification flamed in my cheeks.

"Good morning, Cassie."

"Morning. How are the stitches?" I hoped to divert any uncomfortable questions by bringing up a safer topic first.

"They itch."

He pulled back the sleeve of his shirt to show me a set of twenty-two on his forearm. The skin looked a healthy grey that matched his face.

"Based on Ghua's stitches, we should be able to remove them in six days. We'll watch the skin, and if it looks like it's starting to grow over, we'll cut them out earlier."

"Good." He set a map on the table. It showed Parsons in all its small-town glory. "Will you show us the route we'll take today?"

I studied the map for a moment and pointed to the address Lee had given me the night we left.

"I think coming down 59 from the north will be less risky than trying to come in from the east. East is where the majority of the stores are." It was also where my home was.

He grunted and looked at the map.

"This is all houses," I said, circling my finger. "Train tracks almost split the town in half, and there's more houses on the other side."

"We will stop the truck here and go in on foot." He looked up at the map, and I found the other two wounded fey just behind me.

"Bauts. Azio. You will stay with the truck. Choose two others to guard it with you."

They grunted their acknowledgement and walked off. I wolfed down the rest of my breakfast, not wanting to be the one to hold things up.

Kerr took the bowl from me and placed it in the sink.

"Are you ready to find your son?" he asked when he turned to face me.

I nodded, too afraid to speak, and followed him outside. Most of the fey were already out in the yard, which had turned into a churned mess of dirt, snow, and blood. I hurried to the truck and found a fresh bottle of water and more snacks waiting for me.

"Be sure to eat and drink as much as you can before we get there. We cannot take anything into town."

"I will." I climbed into my seat, and Kerr closed the door.

For better or for worse, today was the day I'd learn my son's fate.

Squatted in my position behind an abandoned car, I peered over the ledge of snow that dusted the window. A group of infected shuffled our way down the center of the road. My hands shook, and the need to laugh like a madwoman warred with the need to cry. We weren't even in town yet. This was one of the suburbs on the outskirts. How were we ever going to get through all of the infected?

The warm, steady presence of Kerr's hand on my back was the only thing keeping me in place. While Kerr and I hid behind the car, many of the fey were spread out, standing still beside trees or a few houses. The infected didn't seem to notice the big, grey men as long as they were quiet and didn't move.

I swallowed hard and watched the first group of infected pass the bumper of the car so closely they could have smelled me if they had any sense of smell.

It wasn't until half of the dozen infected had passed the car that the fey made their move. In a rush, the fey swarmed the infected. A tossed head hit the siding of a nearby house. The thunk echoed in the cold along with the shuffle and scrape of the brief struggle.

When silence reined again, a pile of headless bodies lay in the road. Some weird part of me wondered just how long it would remain there. Probably forever.

As soon as Molev gave the signal, I straightened away from the car and made a dash for the next protective object. Molev and Kerr stayed close to me.

Sprint by sprint, cover by cover, we slowly progressed through the northernmost houses. The further in we drew, the more infected we saw. The smarter the infected seemed, too.

One stopped shuffling and looked at a fey standing beside a tree. It let out a low moan, stopping the other nearby infected. The fey dealt with them quickly before they could draw more infected in. However, that the fey had been noticed meant we had to move slower so every fey could find cover as well.

When the number of infected grew too many to avoid, we broke into a house and waited a few minutes for the group to pass. I looked at the blood-spattered walls and could vividly imagine the horrors that had happened here. It probably hadn't been much different from what had happened in my neighborhood.

One Hound. One bite. One neighborhood at a time. It had probably taken the hound less than an hour to pepper Parsons with the first string of infected that, in turn, continued to spread the disease like wildfire. I remembered hearing screams and seeing Mrs. Hestel wander around outside afterward. I'd almost opened the door for her, but the way she'd moved and the way her arm had hung oddly at her side had made me hesitate. And, in that moment of hesitation, the sound of the knob jostling in my hand had been enough to draw her attention. The sight of her milky-white, clouded eyes had brought the reality of the situation home. That had been the moment I'd known nothing would be okay ever again.

Kerr held me securely as we left the house with the rest of the fey. I quietly pointed which way we needed to go next. It wasn't far now. Although I knew the address and general location of Lee's girlfriend, I had never driven by and had no idea what her house looked like. Seeing a large apartment building in place of a house at the address he'd given almost broke me. There were only so many places to hide in a small apartment.

Swallowing down my fears, I brought my lips close to Kerr's ear.

"That's the building we need."

Kerr motioned to the others. The first group of fey went inside, and I waited with my heart racing. The men all knew what we were looking for. An infant. I'd explained that Caden would be smaller than Timmy. The fey had never seen one smaller and had promised if they found an infected that small, they would not take its head off. They would bring it to me. Just thinking of what they might bring made me want to throw up.

Instead of emerging with a tiny, infected infant, a fey stuck his arm out a window and waved us in. Kerr dashed forward along with the rest.

Inside, bloody handprints smeared the walls. Some apartment doors stood open. Others were closed and needed to be kicked in.

Apartment by apartment, the fey searched for infected.

They found a few hiding in the open apartments. Three guys and two women. As I watched the heads being removed, I wondered if one of the women might be Lee's girlfriend. I still remembered the excitement in his eyes when he told me her name. Dawnn—with two n's—like it made her even more special. It was wrong to hate someone I'd never met. But, I did.

It wasn't until the second apartment on the third floor that I found what I was looking for. Not in the form of a body but in the form of a picture. A picture of Caden, taken when he was six months old, lay on the counter, the edges slightly worn.

I snatched up the photo and stared at it with shaking hands.

"This is it. Her apartment."

The fey checked everywhere on the third floor but found no sign of Lee or my son.

I sat on a kitchen chair and struggled not to cry.

"I knew this could be a possibility. That I'd get here and find nothing." I stared at the picture of my son and let the grief wash through me. He was gone. I was lucky to even have the picture I held. I cried for a moment then tried to let go of my pain. I had a daughter who needed me. I needed to move on. I knew it.

"May I see the picture?" Molev asked.

I handed over my precious memory and wiped my face. The fey gathered around and stared unblinkingly at Caden's image.

"He is very small," Kerr said, taking the picture from Molev.

"They come out even smaller," I said. "Between six to eight pounds is the average. Caden was seven pounds and three ounces. About this big." I moved my arms like I was holding a newborn. The move just intensified my pain. I knew it wouldn't last forever. That the soul crushing weight of grief would lift by degrees with each passing day. Knowing that didn't help, though. I hugged my arms around myself.

"They are so helpless at first. So perfectly dependent and in need of love. And, they give it in return with each tiny movement."

"Where should we go now, Cassie?" Molev asked.

"Back to the truck, I guess." The pain in my chest overwhelmed me, and I struggled to breathe through my silent tears.

"We are not done looking for your son or husband," Kerr said.

I lifted my tear-streaked face up to find a room full of fey nodding in agreement.

"There is much left to check."

He held out his hand, a lifeline to escape my pain.

CHAPTER FOURTEEN

"IF THEY ARE NOT HERE, WHERE ELSE WOULD THEY GO?" Molev asked.

"I don't know. I knew nothing about Lee's relationship with his girlfriend."

"Most humans would try to run away from the infected," Kerr said. "They would go somewhere they thought safe."

I considered the places Lee might consider safe and came up blank. I tried a different angle. If Lee got it in his head that Parsons wasn't safe anymore and wanted to leave, what would he do first? I needed to keep in mind that he had our infant son with him.

"I think he would try to go to our house," I said. "Not because it's safe but because he only had an overnight bag for Caden. Babies need way more than a mostly empty formula container and a change of clothes. And, our house is on the way out of town."

"Which direction?" Molev asked.

"East, toward the business district."

Molev grunted.

Kerr picked me up, and we began the retreat from the building.

It was another hour of playing hide and seek with the infected before I noticed something odd. Every herd of infected that we had come across since leaving the apartment had been heading east with us. Why?

I watched the next group of infected move past then tapped on Kerr's shoulder. He leaned down so I could whisper in his ear.

"They're all going in the same direction," I said.

The wind gusted from the east, and for a moment, I thought I heard talking.

I knew I wasn't the only one to hear it when the fey veered toward a house with a fenced-in yard, somewhere safe to speak quietly.

"What was that?" I whispered once we were inside the home.

"It sounded like a human speaking," Molev said.

My heart started to thump faster. No way in hell did I think that Lee was dumb enough to be out there broadcasting his whereabouts. But, it was someone. And there was a slim chance that someone might know what happened to Lee and Caden. I wasn't sure I'd be able to trust any information we obtained, though.

"Who would be that stupid? Anyone still alive has to know that infected are drawn to sound," I said.

"And light," Kerr added.

I wished he'd kept that to himself. As soon as I had that thought, I mentally slapped myself. No. I needed to know all the dangers. Even if it jacked up my level of terror. How else could I keep Lilly safe?

"I need three volunteers to scout ahead," Molev said.

I shook my head. "If it's humans, we should stick together. The humans here won't know about you. One glimpse, and they'll run in terror. Or worse, they'll have guns and try shooting you. They should see you with me so I can vouch for you, and we can hopefully avoid both situations."

Molev grunted and motioned for the door. I figured that was an agreement when the fey began leaving the house.

The sun rose higher in the sky as we slowly progressed east. Above the continuing sounds of the voice, I heard the murmur of infected groans and the occasional pop. Why would people draw the infected toward their location?

Molev signaled something. One moment we were running between houses almost to the edge of town. The next, the fey were jumping onto rooftops. Kerr crouched low with me and together we peered over the roof. Through the barren trees, I saw a legion of infected and the humans purposely drawing them in.

A barbed wire fence, strung at least ten feet high, ran north to south along Pratt Road, cutting off our way to my house. Infected were tangled in the lower wires, creating more of a barrier for the ones behind them. Beyond the first line of fence, another one ran parallel on the opposite side of the road.

Between the wired lines, a group of people, armed to the teeth, sat on top of a tank. A man with a megaphone was speaking to the infected, telling them to come closer if they wanted a bite of human.

"This doesn't make sense," I said softly, wedged between Molev and Kerr. "Why would people trap themselves like that?"

"They are not trapped." Molev pointed north and south. "They are on the road and can leave as soon as they have all the infected where they want them."

"But why do they want infected there?"

He grunted then slid off the roof without another word. No one else moved to leave, though. Focusing on the road, I counted the humans. There were at least two dozen. All armed with rifles. One man, located beside the megaphone guy on top of the tank, had something bigger. That weapon looked like a mini-cannon.

A minute later, Molev returned to the roof. He held several ball caps.

"Shax, Tor, Gyirk. Will you go with Kerr and protect Cassie while she tries to talk to these humans?"

They nodded, and he handed them each a hat.

"Keep her safe," he said before looking at me. "The rest of us will be close."

Kerr slipped the hat on over his head. It didn't do much to disguise him. He still looked very fey to me. I gently tucked the tips of his ears underneath the hat and used his hair to cover them as well. When I looked at his eyes, they were dilated again. A flush crept into my cheeks at how much he seemed to really like it whenever I touched him.

"It makes you look more human," I said. "Tucking the ears in."

The other three did the same.

Without any warning, Kerr scooped me up and jumped from the roof. He landed with a soft thud, and I looked around, fearing a random infected spotting us. But I needn't have worried. Other fey were fanning out around us, creating a widening circle of safety.

Kerr ran with me toward the road with Shax, Tor, and Gyirk close by. Molev and the rest split off and disappeared between the houses before we passed the final home.

Trees dotted the side of the road, nothing that offered any real protection.

"We can't get too close," I said softly. "The infected are going to hear us."

"No," Kerr said, "they will see us. You will need to speak quickly when we're close enough."

He continued forward. Any infected shambling on the road, the fey killed but not with their usual style. They didn't toss the heads they ripped off, in their typical display of strength. Instead, the fey pushed each body so head and body fell to the ground at the same time. With how quickly they moved, no one would know how they were killing the infected. That the fey knew to be more subtle with their strength around new humans surprised me.

I started waving my arms to gain the attention of the armed men when we were within 500 feet of the fence.

"What do we have here?" Megaphone-Man blared. "Actual survivors? Welcome to our little gathering. You might have a hard time joining us, though." He chuckled like he was the funniest thing on Earth.

Kerr's hand twitched on my leg, and I patted his back, my attention not wavering from the man with the megaphone. With the man still watching us, I gestured at the infected then shrugged to indicate I had no idea how to get around the infected he'd gathered.

"You'll need to head south. It'll take you at least a mile to catch up to the guys laying out the fence. And you better not lead any infected to them. They got work to do, and saving your asses isn't on their list."

While I considered heading south as he suggested, I heard the sound of an engine coming from the north. My gaze tracked the sound and found our supply truck coming down the road between the fences.

"Looks like Tom-man found us another vehicle to use to gather supplies. Good timing."

I watched the truck come to a stop near the tank. A young man hopped out, a dark knit cap covering most of his blonde hair.

"You are not going to believe the shit I found," he said loudly enough that we heard, too. "Not only is this truck half full of supplies, but I also knocked out four aliens to steal it."

"Bullshit," Megaphone-Man said. "Are you taking something again? We need you alert, not high."

How had he gotten the truck? There was no way a single human had stood up to four fey.

"They're not aliens," I yelled, gaining their attention and the attention of the infected at the back of the horde crowding the fence.

"And those supplies are ours."

The guy with the megaphone laughed.

"If they were yours, they're not yours anymore. And how dumb are you to shout with infected around?"

A few of the infected broke away from the group and started to shamble our way. I started talking fast like Kerr had suggested.

"I'm serious. The truck is ours. I drove it here and parked it north of town on 59."

Megaphone-Man glanced at the driver, who shrugged and nodded.

"We need those supplies for the survivors at Whiteman Military Base. We only came here because—"

"I don't give a flying fuck who you need it for, and I know damn well why you're here," Megaphone-Man said. "The world's changed, babe, if you haven't noticed. And it's finders keepers now. If you want to live, haul your ass south, get out of the fence, and find yourself some new supplies in some other town. Everything in Parsons is ours. We're the ones with the weapons."

"What do you want us to do, Cassie?" Kerr asked.

"We need to check on Bauts, Azio, and the rest we left behind. I hate that we have to lose all those supplies, but they're not giving us much of a choice. Like he said, they're the ones with the weapons."

"We will not lose the supplies." Kerr nodded to our

companions.

Shax, Tor, and Gyirk took off with a speed that astounded me. As they ran for the fence, they beheaded infected along the way.

The guy with the megaphone swore, dropped his device, and lifted the gun that had been hanging from his shoulder. Kerr quickly turned so his back was to the man, protecting me.

A single shot rang out, and I peeked over Kerr's shoulder as he ran for the cover of a nearby tree. The men inside the fence all had their guns pointed at the three fey. The air filled with rapid pops, regaining all the infecteds' attention.

He stepped behind the tree, blocking my view of what was happening.

"They're going to get hurt," I said as I grabbed his face to get his attention.

"We will not kill the humans. And, we will try not to hurt them as we remove their weapons. Eden already told us there are too few humans left to kill more."

"I was talking about our friends. Screw the guys on the tank. They obviously have no morals."

"All will be well, Cassie," Molev said from behind me.

I yipped and tore my gaze from Kerr's. More fey were running past us, pouring from the sparse cover of the trees and racing toward the fence. They didn't stop to kill the infected but used the ones near the fence as springboards to jump cleanly over the wire.

The humans on the road screamed and scrambled as the

fey landed in their domain. I watched a fey rip a rifle out of a man's grip and bend the barrel.

"Oh, they shouldn't destroy the guns. We need them."

"Why?" Molev asked. "Guns are only used to kill other humans and us."

He had a point.

"Destroy away."

Within minutes, most of the humans were knocked out cold and all of them divested of their weapons.

Once more, I found myself surrounded by fey as Kerr started toward the fence. Like the others had, he used infected bodies to springboard over it. Once inside the protective barrier, he set me on my feet.

The few healthy humans, who were still conscious, leaned against the tank. Three men and a woman. The men looked winded but angry and still ready to fight. The woman was hard to read. She watched me closely without a hint of fear in her pale blue eyes. I wondered how a woman held her own with such a group of assholes.

"Have there been any other survivors who have come out of Parsons since you've been here?" I asked her.

The guy who had held the megaphone laughed.

"The smart ones got out as soon as the attacks began. How is it that you're still alive?"

"I was one of the lucky few picked up by a military evacuation effort on this end of town. They wouldn't go any further in. Too many infected."

"What are they?" the woman asked. Her gaze slid over

Kerr's face then drifted to Molev, who was standing beside me.

"Friends," I said. "And part of the reason I'm still alive. I'm looking for my son and husband. They'd be easy to spot because my son isn't even a year old yet."

"Babies die," the man said. "Sorry lady."

He sounded anything but sorry. But, I knew he was right.

I looked at Molev. He met my gaze and said nothing. The decision of what to do next was on me.

"A group should take the truck back to where it was and look for the others. The rest of us can keep going."

"The hell you will," Megaphone-Man said. "Those supplies are ours."

I faced the man.

"You don't have any weapons anymore. And, I have more people."

"We have a tank. I think that trumps your freak show. We'll let you pass, but anything you find on the other side of the fence, you bring back to us."

I glanced at Molev again.

"That barrel sticking out of the top of the tank is what fires things, I think."

Molev sprang onto the top of the tank and squeezed the end of the barrel, not quite crushing it flat but denting it enough that it wouldn't fire anything.

Megaphone-Man swore.

"Anything I find in there will belong to my frightened four-year-old daughter who I left behind at Whiteman. Not you."

"You can't just come in here and steal our supplies after we've already established a territory."

"Wasn't it you who said it's a finders keepers world. If you want to live, you better get in that tank and haul ass toward the guys putting up the fence."

"You're going to get yours. Maybe not today but someday. We're not the only survivors, and you're going to need to fight for what you have."

His words didn't scare me. Instead, they gave me hope again. If these guys were alive, Lee had a chance. A small one, granted. But still a chance.

I looked at Kerr.

"I'm ready when you are."

Kerr scooped me up, and Molev gave the signal. The forerunners began jumping over the east fence. The infected on that side moved much faster and swarmed the fey. The fey were strong, but I knew that they could be hurt, too.

Kerr seemed to sense my concern because he held me a little closer.

"You're never going to make it," the woman said, drawing my attention. "There's a reason we put up a fence on both sides."

She didn't say it with malice, just a warning given in a friendly enough tone. I studied her, trying again to guess why she was with that group.

"I have more confidence than you do and better company."

"We'll see."

Focusing on the fey on the other side of the fence, I saw

that they weren't having as easy of a time against the infected on the east side. These infected were smarter. They worked together to try to bite or bring down the fey. The infected still didn't stand much of a chance, though. Heads flew in random directions. One landed at the feet of the woman watching me. Her gaze flicked to it then back up to me, and she said nothing. No one could be that detached.

"You could come with us," I said to her.

"I think I'll stay where I am." Her gaze shifted to Molev, who was watching her closely.

I opened my mouth to tell her that she had nothing to fear from the fey. However, Megaphone-Man's all too alert gaze had me changing my words.

"Suit yourself."

It took the fey a little bit longer to clear a spot on the other side of the fence due to the number of infected there, but as soon as there was a safe place to land, Kerr jumped. The moment his feet hit the ground, he started running.

Excitement built inside of me. I held onto Kerr and watched for the first house that marked our subdivision.

From the other side of the road, a low call rang out. The door of the Wright Signs and Graphics building crashed open and infected poured out. These didn't shamble; they ran. Their smooth, coordinated movement terrified me.

When the first of the infected reached the fey to our right, the infected veered at the last minute. Half of their number ran parallel with us while half went to the left. It was an obvious attempt to surround us, but the fey ran faster, preventing it.

"They're getting too smart," I said softly.

One of the infected turned its head at the sound of my voice and met my gaze. Its eyes were almost clear, the brown of its irises easily discernible. As it held my gaze, the thing smiled. I shuddered in Kerr's arms and looked away. Just how smart were they getting? And what were they evolving into?

Seeing their plan thwarted, the infected changed course again and ran straight at the outermost fey.

"Stay together," Molev called.

Our group tightened ranks, but there were so many more of the infected than the fey that those on the right outer edge of our group were soon overwhelmed. Any remaining optimism I had bled away as I watched one of the fey disappear under a crush of infected.

"Faster. Protect Cassie," Molev yelled.

Me? My throat tightened as I stared at the place where the fey had disappeared. Several of the men slowed and separated infected heads from bodies to help.

The core group of fey closed in around us. I tore my gaze from the fight and looked ahead, spotting the first house.

"My house is in there."

Kerr veered to the left, splitting from the group. He ran straight at the house and launched us onto the rooftop at the last second. Without pause, he set me down on the snowy shingles.

"Stay here, Cassie."

He leapt from the roof and ran back to the other fey who formed a protective barrier between the infected and the house. There wasn't enough fey, though. As I watched the fey fight the mass of infected, more infected circled my protectors.

I watched in horror as still more kept coming down the road. Those that went around the fey came to a stop at the base of the house and watched me silently.

Without thinking things through, I grabbed a handful of snow, made a ball, and lobbed it at an infected. I knew a snowball couldn't take an infected's head off; I'd hoped, on some level, that it would scare them away.

The snow hit the infected in the face with a wet splat. And, it didn't blink as snow fell from its forehead.

The infected next to the one I hit reached over and touched the snow like he was seeing it for the first time.

A loud call drew my attention to the fey still struggling against the horde. Bodies were heaped around where they stood.

The mass of infected, pushing to get to the fey, had brought the group closer to the house. Close enough to see every detail. Every gory, removed head. Every attempted bite.

Within the crowd, a mop of familiar dark hair stood out. My pulse sped up as I stared, waiting for the face to turn. When it did, I thought I was wrong for two heartbeats. The right side of his face was slightly mangled with bite marks. His jacket sleeve was ripped, too, showing more bites and missing flesh.

Lee was infected. My heart broke into a thousand tiny pieces.

Tears flowed freely. Lee lurched forward, reaching for one of the fey. The fey turned, reaching for Lee's head.

"No," I yelled.

Kerr looked at me, and I pointed to Lee.

"Not that one," Kerr yelled.

With that command, the fey ignored Lee and continue killing other infected. Lee shifted his milky white gaze to me and started shambling my way.

I sobbed and muffled the sound with my fist. It was over then. Lee was dead. Somewhere, Caden was dead, too. I gave up all hope of holding my son just one more time.

Alone on the roof, I rocked as I held myself. I don't know how long I stayed like that before I heard Kerr's voice behind me.

"You are safe, my Cassie."

I twisted to look back at him. He was covered in gore and was marked with a few bites.

"I know."

I sniffed and looked down where the infected lay like fallen domino pieces. Heads and bodies coated the snow. Only one remained standing. Lee. He rocked side to side just below where I sat on the roof. His face upturned; his good eye on me.

"That's him," I said. "That's Lee. I'll never know now. I'll never know what happened to Caden."

I stared at Lee, hating him and pitying him at the same time.

"He was a crappy husband," I said. "But he didn't deserve this. No one does."

I knew what needed to be done, what needed to be said,

and I asked myself again how much one person was meant to endure.

"Just kill him." My voice broke. "I want to go back to Lilly."

Kerr nodded and jumped off the roof.

Less than a second later, Lee was gone.

CHAPTER FIFTEEN

I FELT LIKE I WAS DYING. EVERYTHING INSIDE BLED WITH THE pain of what I'd lost. Dazed, I watched Kerr move a distance away to a patch of untouched snow. His gaze never left mine, his steady look the only thing keeping me connected with what was happening as I slowly fell apart. The deep sorrow reflected in his gaze let me know I wasn't alone, that he was grieving with me like he'd promised.

He scooped up a handful of snow and rubbed his hands clean. He grabbed some more and scrubbed his face and chest. One of the group tossed him a new shirt. It wasn't until then that I realized he'd been without one since jumping off the roof.

As soon as he had all of the infected blood off of him, he walked toward the house.

"I am sorry for your loss, Cassie." As Kerr spoke, two other fey lifted Lee's body. A third reverently set Lee's head upon his chest. The fey carried Lee away.

"Where are they taking him?"

"Mya explained to us that your people do not return the dead to the waters but to the earth. We will return him to the earth for you."

Kerr jumped up onto the roof and held out his arms. Standing on shaky legs, I stumbled toward him. He wrapped me in his arms and let me cry. The gentle brush of his hand over my head had the tears falling faster. As Kerr comforted me, I held on tightly and let the pain consume me.

After several minutes, a numbness settled over me.

"There's nothing left for me here," I said.

I looked north and saw a familiar roofline.

"I'd still like to go to my house, if it's possible. I'd like to take a few pictures back with me. And maybe Lilly's blanket. It might help when I have to tell her—"

The tears I'd thought done started up again. It wasn't the torrential outpouring of pain but rather a slow bleed of my soul.

"Yes, we will go." Kerr picked me up and jumped off the roof.

The fey not burying Lee surrounded us as Kerr ran in the direction I indicated. Most of the houses bore signs of the devastation the world had suffered. A broken window here or there. A bloody hand print on a door or the siding. My house looked as ravaged as I felt. Claw marks scored the siding like hellhounds had tried several times to get in.

I shivered and looked at Kerr.

"Maybe we shouldn't go in."

"You are safe, my Cassie. We will get to your pictures and Lilly's blanket."

A fey tried the front door. Finding it locked, he forced it open.

Why in the hell would Lee lock the house before he left? I could only think of one reason. He'd left Caden behind when he'd gone out for whatever reason. My stomach churned.

"I don't think I can go in there," I said when Kerr stepped forward.

"What is wrong?"

"I just have a bad feeling." More than that, I felt too close to breaking. I didn't know what I would do if I walked into the house and found my son dead because of neglect. I couldn't decide which fate would tear me up more: having my son slowly starve or seeing he'd been infected.

"You are safe," Kerr repeated, moving forward.

Inside, things looked like I remembered leaving them in our rush to escape the madness.

"Where is Lilly's room?" Kerr asked.

"At the top of the stairs."

He nodded for a fey to check the upstairs before taking me there. Lilly's room was untouched, except for the bed, which was once more neatly made. I knew we hadn't left it like that. I ran my hand over the pink blanket, neatly folded on her pillow.

"He did this," I said softly. "Lee. He had come here."

I took the blanket and went to the dresser to get Lilly her clothes. From her closet, I took the winter jacket I had purchased for her in preparation for the upcoming season.

One of the fey handed me a bag, and I put everything inside before going into Caden's room. Things weren't neat there. The drawers were hanging open, clothes lay on the floor, and all the bedding was missing from his crib, including the mattress.

What had Lee been doing?

Leaving the room, I went downstairs and looked for the mattress. As much as I didn't want to find Caden, I had to know what had happened. But, the mattress wasn't anywhere to be found.

I was about to turn around and tell Kerr to have the others look for a mattress when his hands came down on my shoulders to hold me in place. I looked at him in surprise. His head was tilted. Many of the fey around us had stopped moving as well. They were all listening.

"What is it?" I whispered.

"A sound. I have nothing to compare it to."

"Where?" I asked.

One of the fey on the steps pointed up.

I went upstairs and stood still. After several moments, I heard it. A faint mewl like a cat.

"Caden?" I said loudly, unable to help myself.

Over my head, there was a flurry of movement. The attic door in the hallway dropped down, and a gaunt, pale woman peered down at me. She immediately burst into tears.

"Thank God," she said. "I thought we were going to die."

"Dawnn? Are you Dawnn?" Hope was making me shake. She nodded.

"Please tell me you have Caden. Please. Please."

She nodded again and disappeared from view. I grabbed the attic stairs, flipped them down, and cleared the top to see her moving toward the missing mattress. It rested on the insulation in the freezing cold attic. And, Caden now lay on top of it, his little hands flailing weakly.

A sob escaped me as Dawnn picked him up and passed him over. I greedily grabbed him and hugged him close, feeling the chill of his body through his blanket.

He looked much too thin. Just weeks ago, he had been a chubby baby. That child was gone.

I fumbled my way down the stairs into Kerr's arms. I barely noticed as he picked us both up. I was busily unwrapping Caden to look at him. He was pale, a tint of blue to his lips. But other than cold and thin, there wasn't a mark on him.

Wrapping Caden up, I pointed to the kitchen.

"He needs something to eat."

Kerr sat me down on a chair, but I didn't stay sitting. Opening my jacket, I tucked Caden inside and zipped up the front so only his head stuck out. Keeping him supported with one arm, I searched the cupboards but didn't find any formula.

"He needs something to eat," I repeated, feeling desperate.

"We both do," Dawnn said from behind me.

I turned and saw her staring listlessly at the fey. They were staring back.

"Are they going to eat us? Like the infected or those dogs?"

"No. They're friends. Where's the food?"

"There hasn't been food for two days. Lee left to get some more, but he hasn't been back." Her face didn't crumple, but I could see it in her eyes. She knew he was dead.

"He told me to wait here and keep Caden safe. I've been feeding him water bottles."

I looked down at my son and gently touched his cheek.

"We need to go to the shopping center and see if we can find something there."

"Are you insane?"

I glanced at Dawnn's panicked face then Kerr. For the first time, he wasn't watching me. His gaze was locked on Caden. I looked down at my son and saw that his eyes were open. Not focused. Just open.

"Do you think you can get us there?" I asked Kerr.

"Yes."

"We need to go now."

Kerr didn't hesitate to scoop me up. I considered Dawnn, who was staring at me with a healthy mix of frustration and fear.

"One of them will carry you. The rest will keep us safe."

A fey stepped forward.

"May I carry you?" he asked her.

"Yes."

Even though she'd said yes, she flinched when he moved toward her. It didn't stop him, though. The fey lifted her into his arms then looked at me.

I adjusted Caden so he'd be shielded from the cold.

"Ready."

Kerr led the way outside. The fey who hadn't come inside with us waited in the front yard. So did a new pile of headless bodies.

Molev stepped forward.

"Do you have what you wanted?" he asked.

"More." I lifted the blanket covering my son's face. "This is Caden. My son. And that's Dawnn."

Molev didn't look at the other woman. He was too busy studying Caden.

"He is small. And, all humans start out even smaller?" he asked.

"Yes. Remember how I said they needed a lot of care? Caden hasn't eaten in two days. And we didn't find any formula along the way. We need to get him something quickly. There's a store just down the road. If it hasn't been raided, it will have plenty of what we need."

Molev lifted his gaze from Caden and glanced at his men.

"I need five volunteers to protect Cassie and Caden."

Five fey immediately stepped forward and surrounded Kerr and me. I gently patted Caden, trying not to freak out over how lethargic he was.

"We are ready when you are," Molev said, watching me.

I pointed down the road in the direction from which we had come.

The forerunners took off; and Kerr, along with our personal guards and Molev, followed. The rest of the fey surrounded us. Within their protective circle, I felt safe and very grateful. I breathed in Caden's scent and touched my lips to his cheek before covering him again. He wasn't getting any colder. But he wasn't getting warmer, either. I itched to prod the fey to hurry, but they were already running. And while I knew they could go faster, I also understood the danger in doing so. I didn't want to rush into a trap. Not with Caden.

We reached the entrance to the subdivision without running into any more infected. The pile of headless bodies and bloody snow looked horrific. Dawnn made a small noise of pure fear and quickly closed her eyes against the sight.

My gaze went to the mound of dirt and snow not far from the pile, and I kissed the top of Caden's head. Lee might have been a crappy husband, but he'd done everything right when it came to keeping Caden alive. And I would never forget that.

Tearing my gaze from my husband's grave, I silently pointed to the building just across the road that we needed.

The fey moved as one. Graceful and silent. I hoped the store hadn't yet been raided. Or at least, not the baby section. Parsons didn't have a ton of options, and I wanted to get Caden in the truck where there was heat.

Before crossing half of the super center's expansive parking lot, the fey stopped. I alertly focused on the building, waiting for infected to come streaming out. However, the doors to the store remained firmly shut. Everything around us remained quiet and still.

A few snow-covered cars sat in the parking lot closer to the building, and an undisturbed blanket of white stretched out in front of the doors. No footprints indicating an infected presence. I glanced at Kerr. He looked down at Caden then pressed his forehead to mine.

"I will keep you safe. I swear," he said softly.

Molev signaled and ten fey ran forward. We all watched as they pried the front doors open and entered the building. There wasn't a sound once they disappeared into the dim interior. No moans. No scuffles. Nothing. It relieved me on several levels. Perhaps the infected weren't as smart as I had thought. Perhaps they had just been lucky when they'd chosen the prior stores. I mean, why choose the Wright Signs and Graphics building instead of the grocery store?

One of the fey emerged and waved for us. Kerr, Dawnn, and I moved forward within the center of the larger group. Watching those before us disappear into the dark interior sent a shiver of worry through me. The dark was never good.

At first, I couldn't see a thing after coming out of the daylight. However, after a few blinks, my eyes adjusted to the weak light coming from the store's front windows. Everything inside looked undisturbed. The candy selections at each checkout remained nearly full, something Mya would appreciate.

However, it was obvious that the power had gone out long ago. A musty smell, with a hint of rancid underneath, clogged the air. Thankfully, the current temperature was keeping the smell from getting worse.

"Grab those bags," I said pointing to a display of reusable shopping bags near the door. "Take everything that's edible."

The fey grabbed the bags and spread out in the store. A few stayed near the front, collecting the coveted chocolate.

"The supplies we need are down this way," I said, pointing in the direction we needed to go.

"Shh," Dawnn said softly from further behind us.

I ignored her and paid attention to the supplies we passed as our immediate group moved toward the aisle with the infant supplies. The contents of the store would fill the rest of the truck several times over.

"We'll need another truck," I said to Molev. "Big, like the one we have."

He grunted and considered the shelves and the fey surrounding us.

"The six of us will search for what we need. Everyone else will stay in the store until we return." His gaze slid to Caden, then he and the others left.

"Can you put me down?" I asked Kerr.

He hesitated, looked around, then carefully placed me on my feet. I went right for the containers of baby food and found something with banana in it, which I knew Caden liked.

I popped the lid open and moved further down the way to grab a box of infant spoons.

"Would you like me to hold him?" Kerr asked.

"No. I got it." I wasn't letting Caden out of my arms for weeks. Maybe even months.

Dawnn made another shushing noise and wriggled her way out of the arms of the fey holding her. Meanly, I wished the fey would have gone somewhere else with her instead of following.

Ignoring her, I took a bit of banana and touched the food

to Caden's lips. However, he didn't open his mouth. I gently nudged his lips apart, trying to get in enough for him to realize what I was doing. As soon as the flavor hit his tongue, he opened wide, in a hungry piranha-style. I almost cried. I quickly gave him another bite as soon as he swallowed then stopped. I didn't want to feed him too quickly and have him throw everything up. He was too small for that.

"Can you start packing all those little containers?" I asked Kerr, who was watching us closely.

I looked up and down the baby section and thought of Angel.

"Actually, let's just take everything if we can."

Caden squirmed in my arm, and I gave him another quick bite. When I didn't immediately fill his open mouth with another one, he let out a pathetic sounding wail that broke my heart.

"Put your hand over his face," Dawnn said, rushing toward me. "Shut him up."

"What?" I slapped her hand away.

"Stop him. He'll bring more."

The sound of something falling somewhere further back in the store sent Dawnn into a panic. She lunged for me and closed her hand over Caden's mouth and nose. He immediately stopped crying, and I jerked him away in horror. He was breathing and awake. Still visibly upset, but not making a sound.

I looked up at Dawnn, my eyes wide. The shock of truth hit me hard.

"Don't look at me like that," Dawnn whispered harshly.

"I'm the reason he's alive. I didn't have a group of grey protectors. I had Lee and an unheated attic cubby in the middle of winter. If I'd let your baby cry, we would have both been long dead by now. So get off your damn high horse and stop judging me. I never asked for any of this. And for the record, I didn't steal Lee. That asshole hit on me and never told me about a wife or kids until after I was already into him. I wish he would have let me walk away instead of talking me into giving him a chance. Biggest mistake of my life." Tears fell freely down her face.

As I looked at her, my anger turned to guilt. She was right about Caden crying. Hadn't I trained Lilly to be silent, too? She'd been older and had the capacity to understand the danger of sound. Caden wasn't. What would I have done in Dawnn's place?

"I can't imagine the choices you've had to face," I said softly. "I'm sorry, Dawnn. For judging you when you're right. You are the reason my son is still alive. Thank you."

She turned her head from me and wiped at her tears.

"Can we please stop talking now? Everything in this fucking world is attracted to sound."

I looked down at Caden, who was still squirming in my arms, and gave him two more bites of banana sauce.

Dawnn reached out and plucked a jar of rice pudding from the shelf. I didn't try to stop her or suggest she eat something else. Given how malnourished she looked, it was probably the safest choice, anyway. She sipped the contents slowly, and we both watched Kerr place the items from the shelf into his bag.

"Brog, can you find more bags?" he asked when the bag he held was almost full.

The fey who'd carried Dawnn grunted and jogged off.

Something clattered not far away, and Dawnn jumped.

"They're hurrying to gather the supplies," I assured her. "We need everything we can get."

"Shh," Dawnn said softly.

Nodding, I focused on Caden and scooped another bite of banana into his mouth. After counting to ten, I gave him another spoonful. He was so hungry, and it was hard for me to not shove it in as quickly as he would have liked.

We were halfway through the container when Brog returned with more bags.

"There is a pile of full bags near the front of the store. It will fill the truck. We cannot take more."

"Molev will find a second truck," Kerr said. "There will be room."

He and Brog started at the end of the aisle, filling the new bags with everything just as I'd asked.

They'd barely begun when something crashed in the row next to us.

"They need to be quieter."

As Dawnn spoke her last whispered word, Caden's gaze shifted from my face to something above me. I tilted my head, following his gaze.

A silently snarling mass of shadow with glowing red eyes stared down at me from the top shelf.

CHAPTER SIXTEEN

Dawnn screamed, but the creature's focus never shifted from Caden. Its muscles bunched as it crouched low and launched itself at us.

Time slowed. I clutched Caden to me. Fear for Lilly and anger clawed at my insides. We'd made it too far only to end like this. I would not lose Caden now. I stared at the hound's teeth and started to turn my back to it. Dawnn continued to scream. But she was close. Close enough to catch my boy. As I turned, I changed my hold on Caden, preparing to throw him.

A roar filled my ears.

The impact I expected didn't come from behind but from the side. Two arms encircled my waist, knocking me off my feet. But, I didn't fall. Time seemed to slow.

Brog lifted me into his arms, his momentum moving me further away from the hound. I held tightly to Caden. Snarls and grunts filled the air.

"Hellhound," he shouted.

I looked up at Brog's set expression as he started to run. Panic and fear gave everything clarity. Brog meant to leave Kerr alone with the beast in order to save me. I twisted in Brog's arms to look over his shoulder.

Kerr strained against the hound, one bulging arm wrapped around the beast's massive neck. Alone, he would never keep the creature from following us. He would die.

A sound escaped me.

Kerr turned his head and met my gaze. I barely noted the blood that streamed down his face from a gash near his eye. I only saw the love in his eyes. His willingness to give his life to keep me safe.

"I promise," he mouthed.

Tears ran down my cheeks as Brog turned the corner, and I lost sight of Kerr.

There was no doubting what he'd meant with those two words. He would do everything in his power to keep his promise. Even give his life. The thought of losing Kerr struck deeply as the thump of running feet grew louder and more fey converged on the area. I held Caden tightly to my chest as so many ran past us. I hoped they would make it in time.

The shouting and howls grew louder, echoing in the building. Those fey who didn't run to help with the hound gathered at the front of the store where the supplies waited. Half the number watched the door for infected that might be drawn by the noise. The other half surrounded Dawnn, already there in the arms of another fey. He looked completely unsure what to do with the silently sobbing woman.

Brog entered the circle of protection. Shaking in his arms, I stared into the dim interior and listened to the fight. I pictured the hellhound devouring Kerr, bit by bit.

All noise suddenly stopped. I stared down the main aisle, barely breathing as I waited for Kerr to appear. The first fey who walked out of the baby aisle were covered with bites and scrapes, their shirts torn and faces grim.

When Kerr stepped into view, my heart broke. His shirt was completely shredded and barely hanging onto one shoulder. Bites and gashes covered his torso. He had definitely borne the brunt of the hellhound's aggression.

I wiggled myself free of Brog's hold and started for Kerr, desperate to take care of him like he'd been doing for me.

"Do not." Kerr held up one hand along with the command.

I slowed and frowned, a little hurt by his abruptness.

"Why not?"

"I am covered in the hellhound's filth. I will not risk you or Caden."

I looked down at Caden, now alertly watching everything from the safety of my arms, and nodded. It would be foolish to go near Kerr now. Yet, when I looked up, I knew I needed to help.

I studied the large gash near his eye.

"You need stitches." I looked around the store. "There has to be a bathroom around here or somewhere where you can wash up."

"Stay here. I will find it."

Kerr started walking away, and I looked at another fey.

"Go with him, please. He's losing a lot of blood."

He moved to follow Kerr. I opened my mouth to ask one of the other fey to go to the truck for the supplies I would need when I realized the truck wasn't even there. I swore softly under my breath and gently rocked Caden, more to comfort myself than to comfort him.

"Does anyone know where Molev went?" I asked.

Several fey shook their heads.

"The truck has the supplies I need to stitch Kerr up."

"I will go find them," Shax said.

Several other fey went with him, reducing our numbers even more. It worried me since we'd already found one hellhound in the store.

I looked at the nearest fey, Tor.

"Do you think there are more hellhounds in here?"

He shook his head. "I do not. I believe he came from the back room. We checked there and did not see any signs of more than one."

Dawnn made a small noise of fear beside us.

"Let's get you something to drink," I said, looking at her pale face.

I moved a few feet over to the cooler at the start of one of the checkouts. I opened it and studied the lines of warm soda inside. Near the bottom, I spotted a bottle of apple juice and grabbed that.

"Give this a try," I said, handing it to Dawnn.

Dawnn's hands shook as she took her first gulp. I didn't

bother trying to tell her to slow down. She'd figure it out on her own, soon enough. However, to my surprise, after that first gulp, she capped the bottle again.

Kerr returned a short time later, bare from the waist up. The bites and cuts I'd glimpsed under the tattered remains of his shirt didn't look as bad as I'd first thought. Many would still need stitches, though. It was the wound on his face that looked the worst. The sides had even begun to pull further apart.

I winced on his behalf.

"That's not looking very good."

He lowered his gaze and began to look decidedly uncomfortable. It wasn't the kind of uncomfortable that I would've associated with being in pain but, instead, being embarrassed. Rather than publicly asking why my concern embarrassed him, I changed the subject.

"Do you think someone would be willing to go back to the baby aisle and grab a bottle and formula? I'll need it for Caden when we're in the truck."

Kerr grunted and slowly walked off to the section himself. I stared at all the cuts on his back. They were fewer and less severe than those on the front, but I still wanted to cry for him. He didn't look like he had an untouched spot on his upper body. And, his lower half didn't appear unscathed either. The way he took each slow step with a bit of a limp had me wondering what injury lay hidden beneath his pants.

I thought of calling him back and asking someone else to go but didn't want to embarrass him further. Biting my tongue, I continued to rock Caden and planned ahead for how to care for Kerr. Even if I did stitch his face here, we would still need to find some place quickly so I could take care of the rest of him. It would take hours to stitch everything up.

Tor began giving directions for the core group to stay by Dawnn and me while the rest continued to gather up supplies.

As they worked, minutes passed with increasing certainty. I swayed side-to-side, comforting myself and Caden as I watched the slowly fading light out the front windows. Molev needed to hurry up with that truck.

Looking more tired than when he'd left, Kerr returned with a package of bottles and a canister of formula.

"Thank you," I said. Shifting Caden's weight to one arm, I grabbed a water out of the cooler and asked Dawnn to help me make a bottle. Her hands shook so badly that some of the water ended up on the floor.

"How are you doing?" I asked her as I capped off the bottle and gave it a vigorous mix.

"Shaky. Inside and out. It has nothing to do with the damn juice or food, either." Still she opened the juice she'd set aside and took another long swallow.

I gave Caden the bottle and listened to him guzzle it. They were both so hungry.

"Do you want to try something more solid?" I asked Dawnn.

"No. Between this and the pudding, I should be fine."

I turned to ask Kerr if he wanted to try lying on one of the checkout counters when a rumble of noise came from outside the open doors. We turned and watched three large moving trucks roll into the parking lot. A trail of infected followed behind.

Dawnn whimpered and moved closer to me.

Several of the fey surrounding us rushed outside. They let the trucks pass then dealt with the followers. Shifting my focus from the bloody fight, I watched the trucks come to a stop in front of the store.

Molev jumped from the first truck and strode toward the entrance.

"Where did you find those trucks? I asked."

"I went south. The people from the fence had them."

"So you took them?"

He grunted. I didn't really feel too bad for the jerks. After all, they had tried to steal our truck.

"I only took the empty ones."

His gaze shifted from me to Kerr.

"A hellhound was hiding in here," Kerr said as if Molev had asked what had happened. "It was trying to get Caden."

"I need the supplies from our truck to stitch Kerr's face."

"It is not far behind."

Five minutes later, Dawnn was once again holding Caden, and I was prepped to stitch Kerr's face. He sat on a stool someone had found, and I stood between his legs, only inches away. He had insisted I wear gloves and douse his face in rubbing alcohol before starting.

He didn't flinch as I set the first stitch. His gaze remained averted and focused on Caden and Dawnn. Like me, I suspected he didn't fully trust her. Yes, she'd kept my son alive; but she didn't seem stable because of it.

I carefully set the next stitch and noticed the way my fingers trembled. I wasn't so stable myself after the day I'd had.

"I'm not sure how badly this is going to scar when I finish. Honestly, I'm not even sure I'm stitching it correctly. It's deep, and I know doctors sometimes need to do inside stitches, too."

I stopped for a moment and took a deep breath, trying to calm the tremble.

"I wish I knew what I was doing," I admitted.

"You will do fine."

I was glad he wasn't worried about it. But I sure was. It was bad enough that his injuries were because of me in the first place.

I worked in silence, concentrating and doing the best job possible. When I finished, a row of small even stitches stretched about four inches long crossed his face. The line bisected his eyebrow by half an inch and ran along the corner of his eye and down his cheekbone.

I straightened away from Kerr and studied my work.

"How are you doing?" I asked. "Everything still work?"

He blinked as if testing his eye, and I was glad to see everything moved correctly.

I stepped back so he could stand. All the supplies were already gone from the front of the store. While I'd been working, fey had packed the trucks full, using boxes they'd found in the back. Even if we hadn't found anything but

Caden, I would've thought this the most productive trip ever. That I had my son and four truckloads of supplies was a miracle.

Molev came from the back of the store as I stripped off the gloves and used the hand sanitizer that someone had brought me.

"We have everything," he said.

"Can we leave?" Dawnn asked.

Molev looked to me.

"Yes. It's getting too dark in here to keep stitching Kerr. The sun is an hour or two from setting. Too low to give me decent light."

Dawnn handed me Caden, and I kissed the top of his head.

"We need to find somewhere for the night quickly. Somewhere with heat and electricity."

"Can you drive?" Molev asked as he studied Kerr's injuries.

"Yes."

"Good. You will take one of the trucks." Molev assigned Bauts and Azio, the other injured fey, trucks to drive as well. I was glad to see they were okay but made a mental note to do rounds and check them over.

"Wear a shirt so you don't stick to the seat," I told Kerr. "And if something starts bleeding again, stop and have someone get me."

He nodded, not quite meeting my gaze. His sudden subdued behavior was making me worry there was something more wrong with him. My gaze swept over him, trying to find what I might have missed.

"Come on," Dawnn said quietly. "We need to go."

Wanting to do more for Kerr, but knowing she was right, I went out to our truck and got Caden settled on the seat between Dawnn and me. Within moments of closing the doors, we set out north once more.

Molev didn't lead us too far from town. Within thirty minutes of leaving the city limits, he found a house and signaled for me to turn into the driveway.

"What are we doing?" Dawnn asked, sounding panicked.

"Stopping for the night."

"Here?"

I looked at the house, saw a light come on, then glanced at Dawnn in confusion.

"They're making sure it has lights and heat."

"It's in the middle of nowhere. There's nothing around to protect us. The infected will see the light and come. Or worse, the hellhounds will."

I could see her shaking.

"It's okay, Dawnn. I stayed in several houses on the way here. The fey will keep us safe."

My assurance had no effect on her. She continued to breathe rapidly through her mouth, her face growing paler by the second.

I picked up Caden and the diaper bag I'd put together while waiting for our truck to arrive. As soon as I opened the door, a fey was there to help me down. It wasn't Kerr. I accepted the help and waited until I was on the ground to ask him to help Dawnn, too.

"She's panicking and afraid," I said softly. "Be patient with her."

Leaving the fey to deal with Dawnn, I went inside. The interior looked about the same as the exterior. A little rundown and definitely touched by what had happened. But, the fey were working to right everything.

"Where's Kerr?" I asked, not seeing him. His truck had led the caravan and was already parked on the road.

A fey pointed towards the stairs.

I headed up and heard the shower running in the master bathroom. Placing Caden on the neatly made bed, I began to check his diaper. He was more alert as I stripped away his layers and definitely felt warmer.

The door clicked behind me, and I looked up from my semi-naked Caden to view a fully-naked Kerr. I should've been looking at his injuries and determining how many more stitches he would need. However, my gaze was far from clinical as I took in every muscled limb and hard—

My gaze remained locked between his legs. I couldn't look away. He was huge. As I stared, it twitched. My mouth went dry.

With effort, I tore my gaze upward to meet his eyes. It took three swallows before I could speak.

"Can you turn around?" I asked.

He averted his gaze again and turned around. However, instead of holding still so I could look at the injuries on his back, he left the room. I swore under my breath and picked up Caden to follow him.

"Where are you going?" I asked.

Kerr stopped walking and looked over his shoulder at me.

"You do not like how I look. I am leaving as you asked."

"I never said I didn't like how you looked, and I didn't mean for you to leave when I said to turn around."

He reached up and traced his finger in the air over his scar.

"'That does not look good,'" he said, quoting me from when we were in the store.

My heart melted a little bit.

"I meant that the injury looked serious. I was worried for you."

He studied me for a long moment.

"The mark does not bother you?" he asked.

"Of course not. Why should it? "

"I saw the way you looked at Merdon and Thallirin. At their scars. They frightened you. Most women find them unpleasant to look at."

"I don't know about most women, but scars are not the problem. In general, you fey are very intimidating. You're bigger. Stronger. Very intense."

He turned around to face me once more, and I got another eyeful.

"How about you go lie on the bed? I'll get Caden settled then give you a few more stitches."

While he did as I asked, I grabbed a towel from the bathroom. It was a struggle not to blush scarlet as I set it over his waist. I lost the battle when his cock twitched under the covering.

Turning away and giving us both a moment to regroup, I focused on Caden. He didn't show any interest in sitting up on the floor once I had him dressed, so I laid him down on a blanket and closed the bedroom door, preventing him from going anywhere once my back was turned.

Kerr watched me move around the room as I unpacked the supplies I needed from the diaper bag.

"Let's start with the ones that hurt the most," I said, slipping the gloves on.

He pointed to the one just over his heart. It wasn't deep, but it was long, reaching to his nipple.

"Thank you," I said as I bent closer. "For keeping us safe. I'm sorry you were hurt because of us, though."

He reached up and touched my hair. The towel moved again.

"I will always keep you safe."

The heat that had been fading flared in my face again, and instead of seeing the wounds, all I could see was a heavily muscled chest and a man who wanted me beyond measure. My pulse doubled its rhythm, and I struggled to regain the detachment I needed to get my job done.

"It might be better if you don't touch me until the stitches are done. I don't want to sew crooked," I said.

He set his hand on the mattress, but the look in his eyes and the tented towel let me know he was still thinking about touching me.

Seven stitched gashes later, I was done with Kerr's front

and asked him to roll to his stomach. When I reached to hold the towel in place, he caught my left hand. His warm fingers feathered over mine. I held still, craving his touch as much as he craved mine.

His fingers paused over the rings I still wore. His gaze locked with mine. With great care, he slowly removed my wedding band and placed it on the bedside table.

"Now, you are free." He held my gaze for a moment longer before rolling to his stomach and resting his head on his hands.

My heart thundered in my chest as I recalled his words. I would be his once I was no longer married. My insides went crazy as my imagination played with what being his would entail.

With shaking hands, I checked the wound on his back. Nothing needed stitches, but I did bandage a few spots.

The soft sound of sobbing interrupted the growing silence.

"I'll be right back."

I picked Caden up from the floor and opened the door. In the next bedroom, Dawnn was on the bed, bawling her heart out. I felt no anger or frustration toward the woman. Only pity.

"What's wrong?" I asked.

She lifted her head and looked at me.

"What's wrong? What's wrong! I'm here, that's what's wrong. I thought we were going somewhere safe. I'm no better off here than I was back in the attic."

Her tears and near panic weren't making sense to me.

"You're much better off," I said, keeping my voice soothing. "You just don't know it yet. We have food, we have water, and we have medicine."

She shook her head and cried harder into her pillow.

"We're going to die." She was beyond terrified, and it was likely not due to her present circumstance but more due to the trauma of what she'd already endured.

"You need sleep, Dawnn. Would you like me to check if there's something in the supplies that can help you do that?"

"God, yes. Please. Anything to skip tonight."

I went downstairs and asked one of the fey to get the red totes out of the truck, along with the little book that gave information on all the different pills we had picked up. As soon as they set the totes on the table, I started searching for something that would knock Dawnn out. I had several options that not only helped with sleep but anxiety too.

Giving two pills and a glass of water to a random fey, I sent him up with a message that the pills should work but that I was not one hundred percent sure. While he did that, I fixed myself a box of mashed potatoes and fed Caden.

I could tell that Caden was tired, but his appetite kept him eating between each slow blink. Several of the fey passed through the kitchen and paused to watch Caden before continuing on. Without a doubt, my son would be the center of attention for a while.

The fey returned before we finished eating and said Dawnn took the medicine without hesitation. I hoped the pills would do the trick.

After cleaning up Caden and rinsing our dishes, I went back upstairs to check on both of my patients.

Dawnn lay on her bed in the same position as before. She was still trying to quietly cry but seemed a bit calmer.

"I'm sorry for everything you went through, Dawnn. Truly."

"Yeah, well, me too."

I stood there for a minute, debating.

"You saw him, didn't you?" she asked.

I didn't pretend to misunderstand who she meant.

"Yeah. Just outside the subdivision."

She nodded.

"I think that hellhound in the store was the same one that came to the house last night. Caden was hungry, and he started to cry. Just a small sound. But, that's all it took. A single howl came from outside. It was far away, but I knew it had heard Caden. Before dawn, I heard scratching at the front door. I kept Caden quiet, praying for the sun to rise."

I didn't ask how she had kept him quiet. I already knew. If she hadn't—I shuddered to think what would've happened to both of them.

"Get some sleep."

I left her alone and nodded to the fey who were already crowding into the hallway.

In the master bedroom, I closed the door and looked at Kerr. He'd fallen asleep on his stomach where I'd left him. There was plenty of room on the king-size bed. Perfect for Caden and me to join him.

Slipping off my shoes, I settled on the opposite side of the bed and placed Caden between us. Even with the lights on, Caden was out cold within minutes.

Curled on my side, I studied Kerr's sleep-relaxed face. My heart gave a large lurch, and I reached out to gently touch his face.

He opened his eyes and caught my hand.

"Mine."

CHAPTER SEVENTEEN

I woke up disoriented for a moment and looked at the space beside me. Both Kerr and Caden were gone. I lifted my head and blinked several times, trying to focus.

Not far away, I saw Kerr holding Caden close as he spoke softly to my son. My heart squeezed at the sight.

"What's wrong?" I asked.

Kerr looked up at me, one of his braids clutched tightly in Caden's little fist.

"There's nothing wrong. Caden was hungry. I fed him milk like you did. He is happy now but not tired. Neither am I. Close your eyes. Rest, Cassie."

I smiled slightly at the not tired comment. Caden's blinks were slow, but he wouldn't stop staring at Kerr. Likewise, Kerr was completely enchanted by Caden's tiny hand.

"You are small but fiercely strong," Kerr said softly. "No stupid human will survive in your presence once you are grown."

He melted my heart a little with those words and the easy way in which he held Caden.

"If you hold him against you and bounce a little bit, it'll soothe him. He might go back to sleep."

Kerr did as I instructed, and I watched Caden's head drop to Kerr's shoulder. Smiling, I lay down again. I wasn't going to go back to sleep. I just wanted to close my eyes.

WHEN I OPENED my eyes next, I was really hot and sweaty. I lifted my head from Kerr's shoulder and looked at his sleep-relaxed face. He had his arms wrapped around me and one leg over mine. It was cozy. Intimate. With not even an inch between us.

My eyes widened as I realized what was missing, and I pulled back a little, looking for Caden. Thankfully, we weren't smothering my son. But, where was he? I fought not to panic.

"Cassie," a voice said softly from the other side of the room.

I turned my head in the direction of the voice and found Shax sitting in a rocking chair positioned in the corner of the room. He held Caden in his arms as he rocked.

"The small ones are fascinating." He looked up at me. "How do I get one of my own?"

I considered his question seriously for a moment. Would reproduction even be possible for them? They had no females of their own. Minus the skin coloring, the eyes, and the longer teeth I'd glimpsed, they were built like us, though.

"The purpose of intercourse is reproduction. That and pleasure. Given your story, how you've been trapped for thousands of years and reborn so many times, I'm not sure if reproduction would be possible with humans."

"Can I hold him a while longer?" Shax asked after a long pause. Although, his expression hadn't changed with my explanation, I had the feeling I'd just made him incredibly sad.

I nodded and turned back to Kerr. I found his eyes open, watching me. I knew from the light streaming in through the windows that I had slept a full night.

"Were you able to sleep at all?" I asked.

"Yes."

He reached up and moved some hair away from my face. I leaned into the touch and closed my eyes. I honestly wasn't tired any longer, but it was just so comfortable in Kerr's arms. A sigh escaped me when his fingers drifted to my temple and began a soft exploration of my face.

For several minutes, I just enjoyed the feel of being in Kerr's arms.

When I opened my eyes again, he stopped touching my face and gently pressed his forehead against mine.

"I will never move on, Cassie," he said softly.

The rocking chair squeaked just then, a reminder that we had an audience.

"We should probably start out. I'm hoping we can get to Tolerance just after lunch."

Kerr reluctantly released me, and I got out of bed to relieve Shax of Caden duty. Not that the fey seemed to mind holding Caden. Shax didn't look my direction as I approached. He was completely fixated on Caden.

"Thank you for helping take care of him," I said.

Shax stood, handed Caden off to me, and put his hand on top of my son's head.

"Thank you for allowing me to hold him." With a final, gentle stroke of Caden's downy hair, Shax left me alone with Kerr.

The sheets rustled behind me, and I resisted the temptation to turn and look at Kerr in all his glory.

"I'm going to go check on Dawnn. I'll see you downstairs."

However, Dawnn's bed was empty as was the hallway. I went downstairs and found her sitting at the kitchen table, staring down at a bowl of oatmeal.

"How are you doing this morning?" I asked. "Did you sleep well?"

"Better than I have in weeks," she said without looking up.

"Is the food upsetting your stomach?"

"I don't know. This is my second bowl of oatmeal. I'm making myself wait five minutes between bowls."

She looked at the clock on the wall.

"Have you seen Molev around? I want to talk to him about our route home."

"Who is Molev?"

A passing fey stopped.

"Molev is gone," he said.

"What do you mean gone?" I asked.

"He left before the light."

"When is he going to be back?"

"He did not say. He only said that you are in charge."

"In charge of what?" I asked.

"Leading us back to Tolerance."

He nodded and continued out the front door.

"You don't look happy that he's gone," Dawnn said.

"Not really." I sat at the table. "He's their leader. They all listen to him."

"Yesterday, they seemed to listen to you, too."

She had a point there. They did listen to me. It just felt weird leaving without Molev. I wondered if he typically went off on his own.

A noise behind me had me glancing toward the stairway.

Kerr came down dressed in a new set of clothes that ran a little small on him. The long-sleeved shirt hugged him in all the right places, and his sculpted chest kept me from noticing the fit of his sweat pants until the ginormous bulge pinned to his left thigh moved.

Mine. The word echoed in my head as I stared, transfixed by the sight of him.

"Holy shit," Dawnn breathed.

I flushed and struggled to focus on Kerr's face. He watched me intently. I needed to come up with something completely unrelated to where my thoughts continued to linger.

"Molev left," I said. "He didn't say where he was going."

Nervous and needing to move, I went to the stove and

looked inside the pot of oatmeal. Enough remained to feed Caden a bit.

Kerr came up behind me and made a face at the sight of oatmeal. Then, he winced when the stitches beside his eye pulled the skin.

"That's a vicious circle. I don't think you want to be making any facial expressions for a while."

He grunted.

"Are you hungry? There's a lot of canned meat in the second truck. Do you want me to get some for you?" The cool air would do my face some good.

"No. Eat. Feed Caden. We will leave as soon as you are ready."

THE MASHED-UP STEEL and car junk wall that surrounded Tolerance was a sight for sore eyes. I glanced at the sun just passing its zenith, thankful that we had made such great time. With our bellies full and a bottle already mixed, we hadn't needed to stop once we'd started traveling.

"This is Tolerance," I said, rolling to a stop near the barrier.

Dawnn leaned forward and studied the wall the fey had created. During the drive, she hadn't spoken much and still looked pale and terrified. But, she shook less today.

"This is a safe zone?" she asked.

"Not quite. This is the town that the fey created. It is safer than the nearby military safe zone, Whiteman."

I picked up Caden, who was sleeping peacefully between us, and reached for the door handle.

"Are there more of them in there?" she asked.

She'd been watching the fey closely the entire way. How they had killed the infected with ease and how they had moved cars out of the way with very little effort.

"Yes, this is where most of the fey live. They will be taking a large portion of the supplies to Whiteman, though, if you would rather stay there."

"No, I would rather be here." She quickly opened her door and found a fey standing right there, waiting for her.

"Can I help you down, Dawnn?" he asked.

She held out her arms in silent agreement, and he lifted her down. Knowing she would be fine with him, I opened my own door.

Kerr was waiting for me. His face looked much more swollen and darker around the injury than it had yesterday.

"How are you feeling?" I asked as he lifted us down.

"Well. The pain is less today."

He looked at Caden, still in my arms.

"Hold him tightly."

I nodded and Kerr leapt up over the wall, landing with a soft thud on the other side. Mya and Drav waited in the snow. Like Dawnn, Mya looked pale but her face lit up at the sight of Caden in my arms.

"You found him?" she said, moving forward.

I smiled and tilted Caden toward her so she could see his face. She smiled widely.

"I am so happy for you."

"This isn't all I found." I motioned to Dawnn as Kerr set me on my feet.

"This is Dawnn. She was taking care of Caden."

Mya extended her hand. "Welcome to Tolerance, Dawnn."

Dawnn clasped her hand and released it again after a brief moment.

"We also found a ton of chocolate," I said. "You look like you could use some."

Mya nodded and rubbed her head.

"I ate my last piece yesterday. That's why I'm here. To help unload the supplies in hopes that you found something good."

"Better than good," I said. "We cleared out a gas station convenience store and a full grocery store. Molev had to grab three moving trucks to fit it all."

Mya rubbed her hands together.

"I've got this. Why don't you take Dawnn to Mom's and get settled in. I'm sure you're both tired. Let's plan on having dinner together tonight so we can hear about your trip."

I turned to Kerr and reached for his hand. His fingers closed around mine, chasing away the chill.

"Lilly is going to be really excited to see us." I could barely contain my own excitement.

Kerr's gaze shifted away from me to the ground. With his free hand, he reached up and touched his cheek.

"I will help sort supplies to make sure you and Lilly will have enough to eat."

He was so sweet. He probably did want to ensure we had

enough supplies, but he was really bothered by his scar, too. Wanting to give him the time he needed, I gave his hand a light squeeze and released him.

"That sounds good. We will see you at dinner."

I led the way to Julie's house, eager to see Lilly. By the time we got there, Caden was squirming in my arms.

Julie opened the door on the first knock and beamed at Caden.

"May I hold him?"

I handed Caden over and stepped inside, shutting the door after Dawnn followed me into the house. As soon as I had my jacket off, I looked around for Lilly.

Julie chuckled.

"As promised, I have kept Lilly busy. She's at Timmy's. Those two have been nearly inseparable."

"How was she?" I moved to the counter and set the diaper bag on it.

"She was an angel. She wasn't afraid at all after you left. It helped that Jessie allowed the kids to sleep over here. They had a great time with popcorn and movies."

"Thank you so much for taking care of her."

Julie's gaze drifted to Dawnn who had remained by the door without taking off her shoes or jacket.

"I'm sorry. Julie, this is Dawnn, Lee's girlfriend. She kept Caden safe after Lee…"

"Never came back," Dawnn said.

Julie's gaze slid to me. I could see the concern in her eyes.

"Lee was infected."

"I'm so sorry. For both of you."

What a messed-up situation. Two women caring for the same man. But in different ways. I thought of Kerr and wished he was with me.

"It's going to be hard to tell Lilly that her dad is never coming home."

"So don't," Julie said. "She's been through so much, and she's just starting to be a little girl again. If she doesn't ask, don't say anything. When she's older, you can explain. For now, she just needs to feel safe and happy."

I knew Julie was right.

She pinned Dawnn with her steady gaze.

"Take your shoes and jacket off. You're welcome here for as long as you'd like. We have another guestroom. No infected come here. Or the hellhounds. You are safe."

Julie reluctantly handed Caden back to me as I sat down at the kitchen table. Dawnn took a seat too.

"Don't get too comfortable holding that baby," Julie said as she moved away to make us some tea. "It's been ages since I held one. And I bet I'm not the only one who's going to want to pour attention and affection on that little guy."

I kissed the top of his head, knowing she was right. Babies were even more special now.

While we sipped our tea and Julie started dinner, she filled us in on what had been happening in Whiteman. There'd been a few attempts to breach the fence, which wasn't anything new. And the fey were working to rectify Whiteman's firewood shortage.

It wasn't too long until Mya and the other fey joined us.

Even with the growing crowd, it was easy to know the moment Lilly arrived.

"Mommy," she shouted.

I watched her bound into the room with Timmy and the rest of their family not far behind and grinned. She was so much more the girl I remembered from weeks ago. I squatted down to catch her with my free arm and hugged her close. She noticed Caden right away. With a sweetness only a toddler possessed, she leaned forward and whispered something against his forehead and pressed her lips there. Then she looked at me.

"I missed him so much, Mommy."

"Me too, Lilly-bean."

She quickly extracted herself and looked at Julie.

"Are we having any dessert tonight?"

And just like that, I knew Lilly wouldn't ask about her father. It broke my heart a little, but I knew Julie was right. My little girl had dealt with so much already. When she was ready, we'd talk.

In no time, the food was served. People were sitting at the table or in the living room with TV trays. Between talking to the other women and their excitement at seeing Caden, it took a while to realize Kerr hadn't joined us.

Before I could ask Shax, I was pulled off into another conversation. It wasn't until I was safely tucked into bed next to Lilly, with Caden sleeping on the floor in a playpen Julie had discovered in one of the neighborhood houses, that I really started to miss Kerr and wondered what had happened to keep him away.

AFTER TWO DAYS without seeing Kerr, I left Lilly and Caden with Julie and went to his house. His "you're mine" talk echoed in my mind the whole way there, poking at my temper. After his talk about not moving on, I sure as hell was feeling abandoned.

I knocked on the door but no one answered. Feeling intrusive but determined, I reached for the handle and let myself in. Like most of the homes in Tolerance, the door was not locked. There really wasn't much of a point. Infected couldn't get in, and the fey were strong enough to break open any locked door.

Stunned by what I saw, I stepped into the living room and closed the door behind me. Stacks of diapers, containers of baby food, a highchair, a playpen, and even a crib crowded the space.

Shax, who had been hanging around for any opportunity to help with Caden, had told me Kerr was doing supply runs. I'd been disappointed to learn the trips were keeping him away, but I understood. The fey felt responsible for all the humans in Tolerance and Whiteman, not just a select few. I could have overlooked Kerr's absence easily if Shax hadn't added that the trips were short ones and that Kerr returned home every night. It had hurt to find out he was purposely avoiding me.

But now, I understood. They weren't just random supply runs to avoid us. He had been gathering everything we would need, just like he'd said he would the last time I saw him. And, he had created a home for us.

My stomach flipped out with nerves. Was I ready to jump back into a relationship? I wanted to say yes but was so afraid of making a mistake again. Somehow though, every time I thought of Kerr, I didn't see a potential failure. All I saw was a potential future.

But, what if my feelings were due to my desperation to get away from Dawnn?

Every time Caden made a noise at Julie's, Dawnn's eyes went wide and her hands twitched. Her reactions drove me crazy. Julie even asked Dawnn if she would rather stay at one of the open houses, but Dawnn openly admitted that living alone terrified her. And, I had to admit to myself that I wasn't so keen on it either when Julie made the same suggestion to me.

Kerr's house had three bedrooms upstairs. Plenty of room for Lilly, Caden, and me. I took a deep, calming breath and started moving the items from the living room to where they belonged. It was time to settle in and make a life for myself again. With Kerr. I just hoped I wasn't reading the situation wrong and wished for the hundredth time he would just talk to me.

By the time I was finished putting everything away and setting up the crib, it was close to sunset. I looked around the bedrooms one last time, then left.

Julie had dinner waiting on the table when I returned.

"I think it's time we gave you your own space back."

"Oh? You decided to move into the house we painted for you."

I sat down and helped myself to a portion of the stew she'd made.

"Not quite. Kerr has been collecting things for us. I think it's time to give that a try."

Julie smiled kindly.

"I hope it works out for both of you."

"Who is Kerr?" Lilly asked.

"He is the one who braided a bead into your hair. Do you remember?"

"Yes, I like him."

"He has a nice house not far from here. It's big, and only he lives there. We're going to stay with him. You and Caden will both have your own rooms."

She looked at her almost empty plate for a moment.

"I don't want to move away from Timmy," she said, her voice warbling.

"You'll still be close to Timmy," Julie said. Just on the other side of the block. Not far at all. And I think Kerr's house has a bit of a hill in the back yard. Perfect for some sledding."

Lilly's face immediately lit up, and I shot Julie a grateful look.

"Can Timmy have a sleepover at our new house?" Lilly asked.

"Not tonight. But soon. Okay?"

A fork clattered, and I looked over at Dawnn, who was now standing.

"Excuse me."

Without another word, she left the room.

Julie reached over and set a hand on Lilly's head.

"How about you and I go pack your things while Mommy finishes feeding Caden?"

Lilly jumped up from the table and raced to her room.

"Thank you for having us and for taking care of Lilly while I looked for Caden."

"It was my pleasure. Any time you need someone to watch the kids, let me know. It was a joy to have you all here."

Less than ten minutes later, Lilly chirped happily beside me as we walked to Kerr's house at dusk. The car lights were just coming on as I knocked again. There still wasn't an answer.

Shaking my head, I let myself in and found more supplies in the living room. Excitement fluttered in my stomach. He'd seen I'd been here, then. And, he couldn't be far away.

"Let's get settled in," I said.

CHAPTER EIGHTEEN

WITHIN THIRTY MINUTES, CADEN WAS HAPPILY SITTING UP IN his playpen, playing with some toys, and Lilly was contentedly watching a cartoon. I explored the house, looking for anything else that might occupy the kids. There wasn't much beyond the necessities, which was perfectly okay. Rick, Julie's husband, had promised that he would return with some kid toys on the next scavenging trip. As a father of two fully grown adults, he'd know what Lilly and Caden would like.

As I explored, I tried to come to terms with the fact that this would be my home, a place I could call my own. And, I felt safe here. Something I thought I would never feel.

My exploration led me to the master bedroom. There hadn't been any reason to enter it earlier, but I did so now, curious about Kerr.

The rich blue bedding complimented the pale blue walls. Grey and white patterned curtains covered the windows. A dark brown, long dresser occupied one wall. Two nightstands boxed in the bed. There wasn't much in the room, but it was clean and neat. And, it couldn't have been more perfect.

Feeling nosey, I checked the dresser drawers. More women's clothing close to my size were neatly folded on one side. The other side of the dresser held men's clothes about Kerr's size. A very domestic setup that made my pulse jump a little. Bits of doubt and nerves continued to bubble up inside of me and I wished Kerr would hurry up and come home so we could talk.

Leaving the dresser, I moved toward the bathroom and saw a novel on the closest nightstand. A doctor romance. I picked it up, wondering why Kerr hadn't gotten rid of it when he'd moved in. Setting it down, I went to check the bathroom before going back downstairs.

Lilly smiled at me and returned to her movie, which Caden was watching through his playpen. I picked him up, holding him close and giving him all the cuddles and kisses he'd allow.

When Lilly's movie ended, I took both of the kids upstairs. It felt weird getting ready for bed without having actual permission to stay. But, I truly didn't want to go back to Julie's until Kerr decided to show his face again.

Dressed in a tank top and a pair of shorts from the dresser, I snuggled into the large bed to wait for Kerr. The house was quiet and the bed very large. It reminded me of the nights Lee had gone out to be with his girlfriend, leaving me alone with Lilly. I'd felt so very pregnant and unwanted then. That same loneliness crept in again now.

Did I honestly want to spend the rest of my life reliving

that scenario? I rubbed my face and curled on my side. Life was too precious to make a mistake.

Then, I remembered the moment when Kerr had kissed me and growled. The need in every touch. Those moments were real.

And, just like that, I knew it wasn't Kerr who'd been faking but me. I had noticed him the moment I saw him watching me as I stitched up Ghua. The fear I'd felt that I'd blamed on his differences and raw strength had been a lie, a self-deception so I wouldn't fall for another man. I hadn't wanted to set myself up for the level of hurt Lee had caused me. But, life was too short to hesitate out of fear of rejection.

I was done hesitating. Now, I just needed Kerr to come home.

I meant to stay awake, but I was too comfortable and too relaxed.

It felt like only a moment had passed when a soft touch, barely a whisper of contact, woke me. I held still as fingers trailed down my arm from shoulder to elbow. My pulse picked up speed. Kerr had finally come home, and as I'd guessed, he didn't mind me in his bed. Not at all.

I opened my eyes and looked at him. He lay beside me, already under the covers.

"It's about time," I said.

His gaze swept over my face. I could see the hunger there, and it kindled my own. I quickly tamped it down. I needed to set him straight before—

"Why are you here?" he asked. It wasn't said in accusation but uncertainty.

"Because I was tired of waiting for you to show up and ask me to come live with you. I was starting to think you planned on avoiding me forever."

"Never."

I reached up and gently traced the line of stitches that looked well on their way to being healed.

"No matter what you're thinking or what doubts you have, don't leave me alone like that again. It felt too much like you were trying to say goodbye. Moving on."

He closed his eyes, his expression turning to one of pain. The hand resting on my arm clutched at me.

"I will never move on," he said roughly.

"Prove it."

Heart pounding, I leaned forward and gently pressed my lips to his.

For a moment, he did nothing. Then, he growled and gripped me tight. I found myself on my back, pinned against the mattress. The feel of his massive erection branded my thigh.

"Mine," he whispered, his gaze holding mine. "I've waited lifetimes for you, and I'm done waiting."

He kissed me hard, each swipe of his tongue more aggressive and demanding than the last. Caged, all I could do was kiss him back. My hands rested on his shoulders, holding on for dear life.

His hips moved against mine, stealing all rational thought. I wanted Kerr. Needed him.

Desperate for air, I tore my mouth from his and turned my head to the side. Kerr took that as an invitation to kiss his way down the column of my throat. I was panting by the time he reached my collarbone and barely felt it when he began lifting my tank top.

He grunted when he got it high enough to free my breasts. They ached for his attention. Instead of moving to them, he moved lower and kissed my stomach. Too late, I remembered my stretch marks and tried to cover them with my hands. He pulled my hands aside, pinning them against the mattress as he continued to pepper me with kisses.

"I love your marks," he said against my skin. "They show you survived a great battle."

I grinned and fought not to laugh.

"It was a close battle," I said. "I felt I was dying a few times."

His trail of kisses led upward, and my humor vanished the moment his tongue laved my nipple. My hips bucked, and he grunted before repeating what he'd done. My hips bucked again.

When his teeth lightly scraped my skin, I groaned. Impatient, I got up and pulled my top off before he could stop me. He sat back on his heels, giving me a spectacular view of his thick shaft, and watched me shimmy out of my bottoms.

His gaze remained fixed on the strip of hair between my legs.

"You are beautiful," he said.

I grinned.

"You are the sweetest man ever. Come here."

I lowered myself to the mattress and crooked my finger.

Instead of covering me with his body again, he did a face dive between my legs. I squealed and slapped a hand over my mouth to smother any further sound from emerging as his tongue explored every crevice I possessed. I twitched and writhed beneath him.

"Right there," I panted when his tongue moved over my clit. "That's the spot that'll make me come."

"Come?" he said, lifting his head.

"No, don't stop."

"But where are you going?"

I groaned into my hands then propped myself up on my elbows to look down at him.

"Come is slang for orgasm."

"Oh. Yes. Drav told us about that."

"What?"

"He heard about it from an audio book. He was the first to learn women like their pussy's licked."

I stared at him, stupefied.

"I like the taste." He leaned down and dragged his tongue over my folds without looking away. The direct eye contact plus being able to see exactly what he was doing reignited the heat the conversation had almost doused.

"What else do women like?" he asked before repeating the stroke.

"That. A lot of it."

He grunted and flicked the tip of his tongue over my clit again. My eyes rolled back in my head.

"That, too?"

"Yep."

His lips closed over the little nub, and I was lost. Tension coiled in my limbs and stomach with each suckle until everything shattered and I fell apart. I couldn't see straight when I opened my eyes.

"Oh," I breathed. "That was amazing."

Kerr kissed his way up the length of me, stopping to kiss my breasts. When he suckled those, I closed my eyes and relaxed into the sensation.

His mouth left my skin, and his fingers traced over my stretchmarks.

"Do you want to sleep?" he asked.

I opened my eyes and smiled at him.

"No. I'd rather find out what it feels like to have you inside of me." I reached out to stroke the length of him.

His breath hissed out, and he closed his eyes.

"Unless you'd rather sleep."

I leaned forward to kiss his chin.

He growled and lifted himself over me. I blatantly hooked my legs around his hips and nudged him closer until his chest touched mine and I could feel the head of his cock at my entrance.

"Just take it slow, okay? You're a bit bigger than I'm used to."

He kissed me hard, stealing my breath and shifted his weight to one arm. With his free hand, he cupped my cheek. Holding my gaze, he eased forward. The pressure and stretch burned for a moment until he withdrew. When he advanced again, he slid in further. The tight fit meant that I felt every ridge and bump on his shaft. It also meant he hit every good place I possessed. I groaned and arched up into him.

"Again," I panted when he withdrew.

"Mine," he whispered before pressing all the way to the hilt.

I moaned and rotated my hips, grinding against him.

He growled and grabbed my hips. I thought he'd tell me to stop moving. Instead, he held onto me as he set a steady pace. There was no long, slow build of tension this time. When I came, it exploded out of nowhere, the walls of my channel convulsing so hard that Kerr's movement faltered. With a grunt, he thrust again, and I felt his release inside of me. The heat of his cum filled me as his cock continued to jerk. I held on tight, riding the lingering spasms of my own orgasm.

When we both finally stilled, hot and sticky, Kerr pressed a kiss to my temple

"Ghua said that Eden will let Ghua lick her pussy again after they shower. Can we shower?" he asked.

I opened one eye and looked at Kerr.

"You want to go again?"

"Yes. As many times as you will allow. Ghua says that Eden allows three before she needs a nap."

I opened my mouth, ready to tell him he better not trade bedroom stories with any of the other fey then realized it was pointless. I'd seen how lonely and bored they were, wandering around out there. The talk wasn't meant to be disrespectful or done with any hint of malice. It was only something they did to pass the time until they found a woman of their own. And without that talk, Kerr would have never known what to do.

Smiling, I wrapped my arms around Kerr's neck and gave him a long, slow kiss.

"I'm pretty sure we can beat Ghua and Eden's record," I said. "Let's go for four."

A rumble came from his throat as he picked me up.

"We can work on the second round while we're in the shower."

***

I woke up slowly. The warm cocoon of the bed clung to me, making me want to stay there just for five minutes longer.

I stretched out my leg, searching for Kerr, but the space beside me was cool. Frowning, I opened my eyes and saw I was alone. I sat up and winced. My legs hurt and my lady parts needed a "do not disturb" sign for at least two days.

The faint sound of Lilly's voice reached my ears. Moving quietly, I gingerly crept down the hall and found Kerr in the guest bathroom brushing out Lilly's hair.

"Miss Julie put two braids in," Lilly said in all seriousness. "I liked two but I think I could have more like Byllo. He had four in his hair."

"I will put five in your hair."

I smothered my smile. Kerr sure did have a competitive streak. I wondered if it was a fey thing or if he was more competitive than most.

"Thank you, Kerr," Lilly said. "What happened to your face?"

He frowned slightly, and I could see the uncertainty in his gaze.

"He got hurt trying to protect me," I said, stepping forward.

Lilly's gaze flicked between Kerr and me.

"You're very brave. Thank you for keeping my mommy safe."

"What would you like for breakfast?"

"Kerr said he can make pancakes."

"Pancakes it is. I'm going to go check on Caden."

Kerr's gaze lingered on me as I left them. I could see the desire there. Even after four rounds last night, he wanted more. I shivered, torn between wanting more and wondering just how sore I'd be if we tried it.

Shaking my head, I opened the door to Caden's room and found him standing up in his crib. He wasn't making any noise, just holding onto the side and looking around his new room.

In just a handful of days, Caden had changed so much. He was regaining weight by eating like a champ. Prior to the earthquakes, he hadn't needed nightly feedings. But, for the last several nights, he'd woken in the middle of the night, wanting a bottle. I was glad he slept through last night, though.

"Hey, little man," I said picking him up. "You hungry for some breakfast."

"Mum-mum-mum," he said softly, setting his head on my shoulder.

I held him tightly, trying not to cry. He'd been saying mum since six months but had been so quiet the last few days.

"Yep. Mum has you, Caden. You're safe now." I pressed a kiss to the side of his head and turned to go downstairs.

Kerr stood in the doorway, watching us.

Smiling, I walked up to him.

"Did you sleep well?" I asked.

"No. But I did not want to sleep."

I chuckled.

"Yes, I remember. So do my lady bits."

He wrapped his arms around us and set his forehead to Caden's.

"She should not be talking about her lady bits in front of you. I will feed her breakfast than speak with her privately in our bedroom about this. Do not worry, my Caden."

I snorted a laugh.

"You have no intention of talking when you get me back in that bedroom, do you?"

Kerr looked at me, his lips curving in a first ever smile.

"There will be noises. It will be close to talking."

I stood on my toes and gave him a quick kiss.

"Feed me something amazing, then we'll see if I'm up for anymore talking."

CHAPTER NINETEEN

Several car horns blared outside, disturbing our comfortable pancake breakfast in the kitchen.

"What is it?" I asked, looking at Kerr.

"Danger. Take the children upstairs. You will be safe."

He plucked Caden from his highchair and handed him to me. Before I'd made it two steps, someone pounded on the door. Lilly hugged my leg as Kerr answered it. Julie rushed in.

"You need to go to Whiteman," she said, looking at me. "Jessie and Byllo are on their way here with their kids. I'll stay, too."

As she spoke, she took Caden from me.

"What's going on?" I asked.

"Here? Nothing. We're perfectly safe. However, there was an incident at Whiteman. Get your shoes and jacket. You need to go."

Lilly didn't loosen her stranglehold on my leg.

"I don't want you to go, Mommy."

I looked at Lilly's terrified face and picked her up.

"I promised Mr. Davis that I would help them if they needed me. Promises should never be broken."

"But sometimes they are," she said. "Daddy left and never came back."

My heart broke a little for her.

"No, he didn't. But when I left, I came back. And I'll do it again. Do you know why?"

She shook her head, and I pointed to Kerr.

"Because Kerr will keep me safe. He always does."

She looked at Kerr, her bottom lip trembling.

"Do you promise to bring Mommy back?"

"I promise," Kerr said.

"Promises should never be broken," she repeated, her tone full of warning.

"I understand," he said. "I will keep your mommy safe and bring her back before dinner."

Lilly nodded and let go of my leg.

I hurried to get my jacket and boots on then kissed both the kids.

"I'll see you at dinner."

Outside, Eden and Ghua were waiting for us, along with Shax, Tor, and Gyirk.

"What happened at Whiteman?" I asked.

"Some infected breached the fence by throwing trees over it," Eden said, looking worried.

My mouth dropped open.

"How in the hell did they do that?"

"Don't know. They're not that strong. Ghua and I are

going to see if we can figure it out. These three are going to stick around and make sure the kids are safe. Byllo and Jessie will be over with Timmy and Savvy soon, too. Ready?"

I looked at Shax.

"Keep them safe."

He nodded, and Ghua picked Eden up at the same time Kerr swept me off my feet.

In less than a minute, we cleared the wall around Tolerance and were racing toward Whiteman. Infected were all over, but so were the fey.

"Why are they so close?" I asked.

"I don't know," Kerr answered.

"Will the kids be safe?"

"Yes. I promise," he said, weaving through the trees.

He moved so quickly I gave up trying to watch for infected and just hid my face against his chest and listened. A faint clamor of moans and grunts steadily grew in volume. It was a sound I knew well from my time traveling with the fey. They were fighting a horde of infected.

"There," Eden said.

I looked up. My chest clenched in dismay at the sight before us. Just inside the fence, fey fought hard against the onslaught of infected pouring into Whiteman via the two large tree trunks, bare of any branches, laying on top of a crumpled section of the security fence. I shivered as I watched a more agile infected climb over the logs and take off at a sprint once it got inside.

While most of the infected didn't get far, a few of the smarter, faster ones did.

"It looks like they took two of those," Eden said, pointing at a pile of felled trees neatly stacked not far from the fence. "But how?"

"We will find out after the infected are dead," Ghua said.

He ran full out toward the fence, not far from the breach, and jumped cleanly over the top rows of barbed wire. Kerr and I were a second behind them. As soon as his feet hit the ground, he kept running, though. I looked back as Ghua set Eden on her feet. She pulled a firearm from her pocket and joined the other armed survivors shooting at the infected.

"I better not have to remove any bullets from these fey," I said, focusing on Kerr's path.

"They will be careful," he said.

"I meant the humans better take care not to shoot them."

He grunted.

The hangar loomed in the distance, fey and infected fighting just outside the doors. I'd never seen a breach this bad since the fey had joined us.

"How are we going to get in?"

I didn't for a moment think that we wouldn't. Heads were flying at a rapid rate. However, there were some infected hanging back, watching our approach. The spark of awareness in their eyes worried me.

"Through the door," Kerr said.

As I watched, one of the fey pounded on the door and called out Matt's name. Several others split away from the fight and ran toward us. With a guard, we made it to the door just as it swung outward and Kerr ran inside.

The door shut behind us with a bang, and I looked

around the crowded hangar at the people milling around. A fearful energy hung in the air. Softly spoken words, sniffles, and some whimpers blended with the low hum of the overhead lights.

"We're glad you're here, Mrs. Feld," Matt said from behind Kerr.

I tapped Kerr's arm and indicated he should put me down. He did so with obvious reluctance.

On my own two feet, I faced Matt.

"How many are injured?"

He rubbed his hand over his face.

"So far? I have no idea. Anyone with an injury is waiting by the Med-Ward. Some of the fey are still searching the tents for survivors." He glanced at the people inside and lowered his voice. "The infected were on the tents in less than a minute after the siren sounded. They moved so fast."

He looked at Kerr.

"Is Molev on his way?"

"Molev is gone," I said. "He left during our supply trip and didn't say where he was going."

Matt ran a hand through his hair and swore.

"We need more men," Matt said.

"I will let Molev know," Kerr said.

"You need to make the decision for him," Matt said, his tone dropping an octave in his frustration and anger as his volume rose. "It can't wait until Molev returns."

With those words, he just helped me close the door on any lingering guilt I had over leaving the people of Whiteman. Not that I'd really had much guilt after the first night I'd slept in a warm house. And, I certainly had even less after last night's bliss-a-thon. Kerr had a magic way of making me forget everything when we were alone. The magic being his persistent and sly ways to get me out of my clothes. Like stealing them when I was in the shower.

I snorted, and Matt shot me a look.

"Do you think this is funny?" he demanded.

I sighed and felt truly sorry for Whiteman's leader.

"Neither this situation or your desperation is a laughing matter. You don't need more men, Matt, you need a different location. The fence is too weak, and the infected are getting too smart. You need something like Tolerance. A smaller area to guard and a better wall. Something you can defend on your own, if need be."

"What are you saying? The fey are withdrawing their help?"

"No. That's not what I'm saying at all. After staying in Tolerance, I can see why the infected are staying away from it. Yes, it's partly because of the fey presence, but you had that here, too. Like you've noticed, the infected are changing. Getting faster. Some of them are smarter. One smiled at me, Matt. I think some are smart enough to know Tolerance would be too hard for them to breach, and they've broken into Whiteman enough to know it's possible."

Matt's shoulders dropped, and Kerr clapped a hand on one.

"We will help you find a new home, Matt Davis."

Matt's gaze swept over the people in the hangar.

"And until we find one?"

"You will have more men."

"Thank you." With a nod to both of us, he walked away to talk to several people in the crowd.

"Let's see how we can help," I said, already moving in the direction of the Med-Ward.

A line had formed, stretching from the screened opening and along the opposite wall. More than fifty people waited. A familiar pale head with a crown of braids stood out from the rest, and I hurried over to where Angel sat with her back against the wall and her head down on her knees.

"Are you hurt?" I asked, reaching out and touching her leg.

She lifted her head and swiped a dirty, shaky hand over her face. With her other hand, she lifted a bottle of juice to her lips and took a small sip.

"I think I'm fine. My heart's racing, and I can't stop shaking. But I think everything is staying where it's supposed to be," she said.

I nodded.

"I haven't forgotten my promise," I said. "When I've finished up here, I'll come find you."

She nodded and set her head back on her hands. The people nearest to us gave me odd looks. It wasn't until I turned and found Kerr standing behind me that I realized the looks were for him.

"Come on. You can help me," I said, taking him by the hand. "You can ask each of these people if they're injured. Anyone bleeding or with something broken should be brought to me first."

He nodded and moved off to the back of the line, working his way forward as I went to the front.

Most of the people I saw just needed reassurance that they wouldn't become infected because of an open scrape. Those didn't stay in line. A few needed stitches because of a fall or run-in with a tent spike. I addressed those first.

While I worked, we all listened. The fighting continued for a long while before Matt's voice rang out with an all clear. He warned those who wanted to return to their tents that they should go out heavily armed.

"The fey have checked the grounds, but we all know the infected are getting smarter. Don't take any chances. Go out, get what you need to live, and come back here."

"Here? For how long?" someone called out.

"Until it's safe," Matt said.

"It'll never be safe," the woman I was working on said.

I looked up from her ankle. Her tired eyes met mine.

"It will be," I said. "Don't give up hope. Not now when we've made it through so much."

She nodded, but I could see it wasn't really agreement. I hoped Matt would seriously start looking for another place. Whiteman was no longer a safe zone, and that was destroying what was left of humanity's hope.

People began moving around. Some leaving, some settling for the night.

Just before four in the afternoon, I finished with the last patient.

Kerr caught my hand and set his forehead to mine. He'd

been at my side through every minute of every hour, helping like he always did.

"I need to keep my promise to Lilly," he said. "It is time to take you home."

My heart sang hearing those words.

"Home. I like that."

I stood on my toes and kissed him softly. He pulled back and gave me a serious look.

"And when the kids are sleeping, we will need to try again."

"Try again? For what?"

"Ghua said they are up to four times before Eden needs a nap."

I laughed and soundly kissed the man who'd stolen my heart.

EPILOGUE

I SAT WITH MYA IN HER DARKENED LIVING ROOM AS SHE nibbled on a piece of chocolate.

"How'd you get Drav to leave?" I asked. "Kerr hovers when I sneeze. There's no way he'd take a step from my side if I was throwing up."

The throwing up was a new, worrying symptom, as was another small grey mark at the base of her spine.

She chuckled then winced and held her head.

"I told him if he didn't leave, I'd never let him see my pussy again. I think it was the fact that I used the p-word that let him know just how serious I was."

I chuckled.

"They do like using that word, don't they?" I studied her face for a moment longer, wishing I could be more useful. "I'm sorry there's not much I can do for you. Are you sure you don't want to try some of the pills we came back with?"

"No. I'd rather save them for someone who really needs them."

I bit my tongue. If anyone needed them, she did. Most people didn't get accidently hurt anymore. The two scenarios were either healthy or infected, which is why I was so worried about Mya.

"Seriously, you're helping just by being here. I need more distractions like this. Sitting in this house day after day makes it worse."

Distracting conversation I could do.

"Any word from Molev?" I asked.

"No." She set her head back against the couch and closed her eyes. "He's never left like this before, but Drav's completely unconcerned. He keeps reminding me that Molev is the strongest among them because of his damn hair. He doesn't get that he was the strongest in their home, not necessarily here. There's still so much they don't know."

"You're very right about that. Shax asked me how babies are made. He's completely infatuated with Caden."

She smiled but kept her eyes closed.

"A few of them have come to me to ask where they can find babies. I hate telling them there's little chance of finding some alive anymore, Caden being the exception."

We both knew I'd been beyond lucky to find Caden.

Thoughts of babies inspired a new topic.

"Did I tell you about the new girl?"

"Mom did. I'm going to try to go say hello as soon as this headache gives a little."

"Good. I think she's going to fit right in here once she gets comfortable. She's a bit skittish."

Mya chuckled.

"Aren't we all at first?"

"I suppose we are. The fey tend to change that pretty quickly, though. Don't they?"

"They sure do." She sighed and lifted her head to meet my gaze. "Want to go for a walk?"

"Just like that?"

"Yep. Just like that." She stood and stretched. "A bit of chocolate and the headache fades enough that I can function again for a few hours. You should see my cupboard. Drav stole every bit of chocolate that was in the supply shed. There's no real food in this house."

I stood and started getting my coat and boots on.

"There's not much in the supply shed either. Kerr and Drav gave the majority to Whiteman after the attack. They said we have enough to last us the week, but they're planning on putting those extra trucks we have to good use in the next few days."

"Any word from Whiteman?" She pulled up the zipper and reached for the door.

"They're scouting neighborhoods for the move. Matt's looking more high-strung than ever."

"Between you and me, I'm glad there aren't enough homes here to house everyone," Mya said. "After seeing the way the survivors as a whole just wanted to hand over the responsibility of their survival to the fey, I like the separation.

Yes, the fey should help us; it's their curse that broke the world after all. But we need to help ourselves too. Put in some real effort, you know? If we can't, we don't belong here."

I agreed with her. We needed to help ourselves and not abuse the fey's willingness to help us. Yet, there were some things they just wouldn't allow us to do. Well, the females anyway.

Outside, both Kerr and Drav were lingering on the sidewalk. When the door opened, they both froze like guilty kids. I grinned at Kerr.

"Let me guess…Shax is watching the kids?"

"He took them to play at Jessie's house."

That meant we would have the house to ourselves.

"I think I'll take a raincheck on that walk," I said to Mya. She chuckled.

"Given the way Drav's looking at me, I think I'll need to do the same."

Kerr crossed the street and scooped me up into his arms. From the corner of my eye, I saw Drav do the same to Mya, and I almost snorted at his softly worded question.

"Do I still get to see your pussy?"

Kerr started jogging before I could hear her answer.

"In a hurry?" I asked.

Kerr's gaze flicked to my face.

"To be with you? Always."

I smiled and laid my head against his chest. Kerr was the best thing to happen to me.

. . .

THANK you for reading *Demon Deception*! Cassie's story was a bit more serious than Eden's in *Demon Escape*. Rightfully so, given her situation. But, don't worry. *Demon Night*, Angel's story, is gearing up to be much lighter. Keep reading for a sneak peek!

AUTHOR'S NOTE

It was so much fun to take the survivors out of their comfort zone and show what's happening with the infected and in the world. While Eden's story proves it's possible to survive outside of the safe zone, Cassie's story shows just how hard it's getting (giggles) out there. I can't wait to share the next piece (snort) with you. Angel's story is unlike any other!

If you want to keep up to date on my release news, teasers, and special giveaways, please consider subscribing to my newsletter: mjhaag.melissahaag.com/subscribe (I only send periodically, so you won't be overwhelmed.)

Until next time!

Melissa

SNEAK PEEK OF DEMON NIGHT

I ran through the survivor camp with everything I had, one human in a herd of humans trying to escape the infected. The people around me were screaming and yelling, making it harder to hear what was behind us. I didn't try to look. I already knew what the infected looked like. Pale. Cloudy eyes. Missing parts. A craving for human flesh.

A woman tripped on a tent stake and fell in front of me. If I were a better person, I would have stopped and tried to help her up. But I didn't. I couldn't. I'd promised I would do everything in my power to survive, and I would. So, I kept running even as I cramped. Even as every breath sent a stab of pain through my middle.

You can do this, Angel.

Because I knew, if I couldn't, I would die.

Out of nowhere, a fey came running at me.

"Get down!" he yelled.

I fell to my stomach and winced at the wet splattering sound behind me.

"Run," he said.

I hopped to my feet, almost slipping on infected blood slicking the snow around me and ran again. I knew I was covered in infected blood but didn't stop to remove any one of my seven layers. I needed all of them.

Ahead, I spotted the hangar. A beacon of safety.

I made it through to the door with several other winded runners. There was already a crowd of people inside. Cattle waiting for the slaughter if the fey couldn't keep up with the infected pouring in.

One of the grey devils strode past as I walked small circles, trying to cool down from the mad sprint here. Tall, broad-shouldered, and all men, the fey appeared after the earthquakes that were felt around the world several weeks ago. If they were the only thing to appear, we would have been fine. The fey were huge, strong, and like ripping heads off of things, but they had a soft spot for women. Thankfully. Human men they only tolerated.

Too bad the hellhounds came before the fey.

Unable to bear the pain in my middle for a moment longer, I braced my hands on my knees and hoped that belly dive hadn't hurt the baby. At just six months, I didn't have much of a bump yet and had landed mostly on my knees and elbows.

Please just stay where you are, I thought to my stowaway. *Now is not the time for a surprise appearance.*

Not that I thought a few more weeks would make the

world a safer place. Today. Tomorrow. Nine weeks from now. The length of time didn't change the truth of our situation. This baby and I were royally fucked.

Okay...so that doesn't sound lighter, but it is. I promise! Get the scoop about Shax and Angel's rocky road to dating and learn what's up with the rest of the survivors in **Demon Night**.
Big things are coming!
Now available!

Connect with the author

Website: MJHaag.melissahaag.com/

Newsletter: MJHaag.melissahaag.com/subscribe

Lightning Source UK Ltd.
Milton Keynes UK
UKHW011827140420
361682UK00007B/2090

9 781943 051304